# Exiled from Nobu

## A Xiveri Mates Novella

Elizabeth Stephens

# Content

# Pronunciation Guide & Glossary

**Bo'Raku** *(boh - rah - kooh)*
Ruler of the Drakesh planet, Cxrian; once an independent planet,  but following a failed invasion of Nobu, the planet was absorbed into the Voraxian Federation

**Cxrian** *(ss - ree - ahn)*
The red planet, coined for its color as seen from outer space, as well as the red skin tone of its primary species, the Drakesh

**Drakesh** *(draah-kesh)*
Beings of Cxrian that were once autonomous before their failed invasion of Nobu; afterwards, their planet was absorbed into the Voraxian Federation

**Hexa** *(hex - ah)*
Yes

**Kiki** *(kee - kee)*
human name

**Kinan** *(keh - naan)*
Okkari's slave name

**Nobu** *(noh - boo)*
Voraxia's largest planet; ruled by Va'Raku; characterized by icy climates and long, brutal winters

**Nox** *(noh - cks)*
No

**Okkari** *(oh - car - ee)*
Principle warrior and traditional ruler of Nobu; see Va'Raku for alternate title in the Voraxian heirarchy

**Va'Raku** *(va - rah - kooh)*
Ruler of the Voraxian planet, Nobu, as decreed by Voraxian heirarchy; see *Okkari* for alternate definition

**Va'Rakukanna** *(va - rah - kooh - kah - nah)*
Mate of Va'Raku; see *Xhea* for alternate definition

**Verax** *(vair - axe)*
Explain

**Voraxia** *(voh - racks - ee - uh)*
Chief planet of the Voraxian Federation; base of the Raku; characterized by expansive werro woodlands and a sandy forest floor

**Xhea** *(shay - uh)*
Mate of the Okkari; see Va'Rakukanna for alternate title in the Voraxian heirarchy

**Xok** *('ok) or (tzok)*
Curse word used universally and liberally

**Xora** *('oh-ruh) or (tzoh - ruh)*
Cock, dick, penis, or your word of choice for it

To Ahmaud Arbery.
Rest among the stars.

elizabeth

# 1

## Lisbel

We watch each other across the space.

It's small. Filthy. Everything's covered in a thick layer of red dust. It's nothing at all like the large dome I left behind on my ice and snow-covered home, Nobu. Nox. This has nothing to do with Nobu. This little moon is covered in visible dirt, with the exception of a few black screa hills that would shred the soles of my feet right open if I dared to walk on them without shoes. Without *sandals.* That's what the humans call these flimsy foot covers.

Of course, I have more toes than they do, so I had to stuff my feet into these strappy things. My...the male who lives in this dirt house with me helped me create better straps out of reeds. Reeds. Like there is no technology. Like we aren't even within Voraxia anymore. Where are the Hogers who can make clothes custom to fit even the tallest form? Where are the Evras who can make foods for me to eat?

Where are the Xcleranx who can fight and defend me from the khrui monsters that roam ever closer to the Droherion Dome that protects this filthy human colony

— or even worse, the filthy humans *beneath* the Dome who I am supposed to be making a new life among?

In exile.

I often feel like running out of this shack that my — that *the* male calls a home and heading for those screa cliffs. I'd have better luck making a home among those wretched khrui beasts that roam this moon than I would among the humans.

How did it come to this?

*The cold winds thrash and burn, but no more than usual. What burns is the knowledge that I'm on trial for crimes that I knowingly committed against the Okkari of Nobu, its ruler. I can't fight. I always wanted to learn, but my sires never allowed it. Females are too rare in Voraxia to risk allowing them into combat. Females can never be warriors. At least... that's what I believed my whole life.*

*My whole life, I've been wrong.*

*I've seen female warriors fight. Watched it with my own eyes. If such a battle hadn't ended moments ago, I'd have never believed it myself. And now I stand before warriors — male warriors and female ones — knowing that I am a criminal and knowing that I wouldn't have the strength to defend myself even if I tried.*

*I am humiliated. The sensation is almost enough to take me to my knees. Almost. Because there is a sensation that is miraculously stronger than this one keeping me upright. Nox. Not upright. Making me weightless. I weigh nothing against it.*

*I can feel a tugging in my chest, begging me to turn around. I do, and that's when I hear a groan. I don't understand the sound as I hear it, because it reverberates with tension and fear and, above all other things, lust. To call the voice male would be an injustice. It's like the universe, Xana,* is speaking directly into my ear, telling me her secrets. It's like my soul, Xaneru, mate to Xana, has reached for a box inside my belly I did not know existed and unlocked it and let every emotion I didn't know I was capable of, rampage through me in the same moment.

I start to shake as I scan the crowd looking in on me, searching, searching, searching…"Fuck the sun," comes the curse in a language I can only understand because of the translation implant given to me, "I'll champion for her."

My gaze narrows on a kneeling form. As he rises, I can't believe what I see. He has dark brown skin, a shade that is not Voraxian or shared by any other species I have ever seen. His hair falls in thin ropes down his back. His eyes are just as bleak as they are black when they look up at me.

I don't understand. This is a human. And worse, this human looks at me like he despises me. He can't possibly be my… "Are you…" But I don't need to ask. I know that this human that I hate and that hates me equally is the male that the fates chose for me. He is my biological match, the one with whom procreating will be possible. Perhaps the only male with whom it can be.

He is my Xiveri Mate.

I know that he is, like I know my true name is Lisbel. Like I know the cold and the ice and the darkness that is my home. Like I know that more than anything in the world, all I have ever wanted is to be a queen and a warrior and now I never will be because my mate is a human who hates me.

"Yeah," he says, speaking like it causes him great pain. I cannot truly tell. We Voraxians wear our emotions in the colorful ridges that dot our forehead in the same place these humans have 'eyebrows.' "I'm your Ziv-whatever. Your mate. You're not fighting today, and you're not going into exile."

I didn't fight that day, but I did go into exile. I'm not sure if the human advisor called *Svera* responsible for this decision is the kindest creature I've ever met or the most sinister. Because instead of exiling me to the great white ocean where all those on Nobu are exiled — essentially, sentenced to death — she had me exiled here, to the human moon colony where I am the only alien among them and the only creature on whom I can rely is a human warrior male who thinks me disgusting even though he is bound to me for life.

"You hungry?" He says in his language, standing up from the wooden table in the center of the eating room he calls *kitch-nn*.

"Nox," I answer in my own language, ignoring the pull in my gut at the sight of his bare chest covered in a sheen of sweat because here it is always hot.

"Haven't eaten this solar."

"I don't need to eat every solar. My body is more efficient than yours. It needs less sustenance and I generate less waste." I wait for him to look at me and acknowledge the insult, but he doesn't and it annoys me more than it should.

It would be better if I could ignore him the way he ignores me. Then I could live out my sentence here in peace instead of being plagued by thoughts of him in the lunar, heat building and blossoming through me that's getting harder and harder to ignore. But from rumors I've heard, the Xanaxana affects our kind far more rapidly and more intensely than theirs. What if he only has an inkling? What if he never feels anything for me at all? *I've given him no reason to...*

"Fine. Going out." He grabs his fighting staff and a sheathed sword from the rack of weapons hanging beside our front door — *the* front door. His long hair he keeps tied back in a leather strap at the nape of his neck. The long, rope-like tips swish against his lower back where there are two subtle indents. I lick my lips. He isn't my kind — he isn't even a ruler among his — but I do seem to like the shape of him.

"Where?" I say as he opens the front door and the miserable sight of this red planet greets me.

I already know the answer. "Training field."

"So you can attempt to redeem yourself after failing on Nobu's ice flats?" It's a low insult, one I've made before.

And it never works. "No. Don't see myself fighting in the snow anytime soon."

He steps through the door.

"Wait."

He waits.

"What should I do?"

"Don't know. Don't care." He doesn't look back at me.

"I won't be here when you return."

"So you've said the past seventeen solars." Seventeen solars. That's how long I've been on this Xana-forsaken rock. That's how many vows I've made to run. That's how many times I've reneged on that suicidal vow.

"Well, I'm not staying here."

He chuffs, looking at me and his eyes are dark and his face is so well formed. *Perhaps, even more well-formed than the Okkari's.* I wince at the thought of how I debased myself with him, of the lies I told the Xhea of Nobu so that I might usurp her place, little knowing that my attempt would bring my own Xiveri Mate onto Nobu's shores. He is a *friend* of hers. I'm not familiar with this concept and I hate the term. It means other females can approach my Xiveri and speak with him, share their true names with him because these humans don't even use titles. And, if his affection for me is so little, perhaps even *lay* with him while I sit here pining after a male I loathe.

"Never told you you had to. In fact, you shouldn't be here. You should be out there gettin' to work. There's lotsa shit to do, helpin' with the construction of the birthing center, or building the new houses."

"I don't build."

"Food's gotta get made. Cooks could always use a hand."

"I don't cook."

He looks at me, long and lingering. "Then do whatever you want."

"I want to leave."

"Not stoppin' you."

"You're hardly a warrior — you can't."

He grins with one side of his mouth and it transforms his face. Utterly spellbinding. "Against a fierce warrior like you? Wouldn't dream of tryin', princess." His wink and his stupid, cavalier grin only serves to make the insult more cutting before he disappears, shutting the door in his wake.

I sit where I've been sitting for seventeen solars — on the small series of poofs and pillows spread out against the front wall beneath a wide window. They form a sort of lounge area — nowhere near so nice as the Okkari's on Nobu, but...quaint. It's also where he sleeps every lunar since I occupy the one bed. *It smells like him here.*

I'm still contemplating what I could have said to insult him worse than he insulted me — because he always seems to hurt me more than I do him even though *I'm* the one trying…it really isn't fair — when someone knocks on our door.

The door.

I jerk up and make the mistake of peering out of the slatted window — because this house, like so many others on this stupid rock, doesn't contain any glass. The female standing there sees me and waves her stupid hand and looks at me with her stupid grin.

"Lisbel?" She says. Her name is Merciful or Mercy or Mary or something silly and I hate that I know her name, but only half so much as I hate that she knows — and so freely uses — mine. "Lisbel, I know you're in there. We could really use your help translating with some of the Voraxian builders. They claim not to have translators."

"It's a lie. Any Voraxian sent here to work will have been equipped with a translator. They pretend not to in order to insult you."

"All the same, we need them to move the foundation beams or…or whatever it is that they're laying down away from the Antikythera Satellite ruins. It's sacred ground for those of us who worship the Tri-God."

"Please! We need you to do the clicking sounds at them and make them go away!" Ugh. The sound of the small kit grates. *Largely, because I have trouble denying her.* The little female is one of a few kits I've ever seen with my own eyes.

I sit up a little taller, peering out through the slats like a robber as I attempt to get a good look at the kit. She is half my height, only two rotations old, capable of speaking in full sentences and expressing herself, though she does occasionally drift off and babble. I'm grateful that the translators were fit to every human, otherwise, I would not be able to understand this one at all.

I smooth down my skirts and open the front door. The little kit with her deep brown skin and cloud of soft brown hair squeals at the sight of me. She tries to rush forward, but her mother holds her back by the arm and with soft admonishments.

"Sorry, but Pluto refused to be left behind when I told her I was coming to see you."

"Mars is going to be *soooo* jealous." She speaks of her *brother*. A concept we, on Nobu, also find alien since our females are known to be capable of producing only one kit in a lifetime. "He thinks you're so pretty. I think it's just because you don't wear a shirt, but mama says…"

Her mother slaps a hand over the youngling's mouth and her face elongates in horror before she manages to recover with a laugh that sounds more like a cough. These humans. Without their ridges their visible reactions are always so strange and over the top. "Sorry about that. Pluto is uhh…"

"A kit," I finish for her.

She smiles more broadly at that and straightens up, passing a hand over her short curls. "Exactly. So…will you come?"

I can't think of one better thing to do and no excuses come to me as I stare down into the kit's face, radiant with enthusiasm. My shoulders slump forward and I sigh, "Take me to the builders."

# 2
## Lisbel

"What do you mean, these were your orders? I know for a fact that they could not be given the amount of indulgence our Raku grants these…these beings. This is a…" I glance over my shoulder at the wreckage Mercury tells me is alleged to be some sort of place of worship. It hardly looks to be more than a few beams with canvas stretched between them, but that is not for me to judge. I will never come to this place to worship anything.

The four Voraxian males surround me, their smirks fixed in place. "A few solars later and the disgraced *Lisbel* already shows her true colors." His gaze flicks to my ridges and I despise him for it.

"Guess that's what xoking a human does to one of ours."

"But do you think his xora's really as small as they say human xoras are? Maybe, she can't even feel it."

They all laugh. "Maybe a good xoking is exactly what she needs."

The male standing just in front of the others looks at me with a brutality that's reflected in his ridges — they choose to flare both red and black when I inhale and roll back my shoulders. I begin to consider that this male might be cosmic scum to allow the colors in his ridges to break in front of me — a female of Nobu — and disgrace himself in such a way. And when he speaks, I'm sure of it.

"When the human xoks you, do you even feel it? Nox, I don't think she does. Not after the gaping cunt the Okkari left behind." The others laugh while rage boils in my blood — shame too, but of the two emotions, rage is the more prominent. And then the male sneers, colors in his ridges flashing freely once more. "But he didn't want you for his Xhea, did he? He found you *repulsive*. Nox, the only male who would ever want you, *Lisbel*, is human."

I step forward, holding my colors in check. "Do you think you can intimidate me?" I will not give them the satisfaction of knowing that of the blows they intended to wound, most of them did. "Do you not know who I am? Where I come from?

"I am of Nobu, a place far harsher and more desolate than anything you younglings, who have lived coddled in the warm womb of Voraxia's capital, could imagine. I have stared down the jowls of a hevarr beast and lived. You may know my born name, but at least you have heard of me. But you?"

I scoff and turn my gaze past this sham of a leader, to the other recruits. "You are trained brutes, too pathetic to ever aspire to anything more than males toiling in the dirt whose only power lies in your perceived superiority, but what is that against my — and all of these humans — very real indifference?

"And you speak of matehood?" I push my hair over my shoulder and just my finger forward, very pleased by the way one of the males jumps, just a little, as if in fear of me. In fear. Of *me.* I look at him as I say, "You four are far, far too pathetic to ever hope to attract a mate, *even* a human one." *Maybe, especially. The humans have survived so much and still speak freely with me, like Mercury and her little kit, Pluto. They honor me.*

"So nox, little younglings, you may continue to use my born name all you like and, while I won't even bother to learn your titles, I will insist that you move your…contraptions to another part of this dreary, miserable stone as these humans rather like their…" I wave my hand dismissively at the wreck of some satellite that has too long and complicated a name to bother with — and the humans forming a shield wall with their own beating hearts before it. "I would not want to have to report you for your insolence."

The males' ridges are flashing now with violence and I smirk smugly, knowing I have won this exchange in that brief slip. To display like this is such a vulgar thing. It's clear they were poorly bred with violence and anger in their hearts. They know nothing of Xanaxana. They know even less of this alien human concept they call *love.*

*And I am…I was…not so distant from them.*

I stare at the leader — a Voraxian with skin that's nearly green in hue — and glare ferociously at his ridges until he quiets them. He reminds me far too much of myself and I feel anger at the thought that I am speaking to myself just a half rotation ago. How abhorrent I was then… *Have I changed much since?* It bothers me that I can't say for sure…

He grunts in the back of his throat, "I am Ru'Gorganox of Voraxia and you, a disgraced female, dare to speak to me like this? I will report *you* to the Raku…"

I throw my head back and laugh, face tilting up towards the sun. "I have already been exiled, xub'Gorgal or whatever you are. Do your worst. And by the way, I never said I would be reporting you to the Raku. I will report you to his Rakukanna — or better yet, to Nobu's Xhea — and we shall see who, between the two of us, makes it out of this with their skin."

The male steps forward, but his *friends* take him by the arms and pull him back. "She isn't worth it," one of them says.

And another. "We're being watched." The Voraxian laborers gathered at the base of the hill along with the other materials have crept closer, likely curious about this exchange. One of them calls up, "We're being called back by Gorganox and the human Council."

"Come. Let's go."

Gogo stands down and moves away from me with one final whispered threat, "This is not over between us, Lisbel."

"I have better things to do with my time than waste it having this conversation again. Move your building blocks, younglings," I shout louder now to the rest of the forty or so Voraxian builders here. They look at me, surprised, but not surprised enough to dare question me again when their leaders grab two opposite ends of an enormous stalyx metal beam and begin toting it back towards the clustered houses that form the majority of this colony.

The only homes worth living in are those built on the hill that rises up in the distance, but my mate is not revered enough to own one of those and for that, I'm rather grateful. I've met the inhabitants of those homes... the well-dressed female who runs this rock and her

Council of cronies and I have found them…lacking, at best. At worst? Frightful.

I turn back to the crowded humans and wave my hand. "Get back to work or prayer or whatever it was you were doing."

But none of them move. They all just stare. If I had the ability to get red in the face as some of the paler skinned humans are so apt to do, I'd likely have done it then. Their expressions I simply cannot make out but uniformly include large, rounded eyeballs, large rounded mouths, fleshy pink tongues waggling within them but saying nothing of help to me.

"Verax," I insist, a term to mean that they should *elaborate*. They don't.

I look to Mercury. "What?" I say in *human*. Ugh. A barbaric language. I can't even believe the word came out of my mouth…

Pluto drops to her knees and clasps both hands beneath her chin. Her eyes light up and tears explode from them and I am about to insist that we call for a healer of some kind to care for the small female who has evidently, lost her small mind, when she releases a belting sob, "Oh my comets! That was the coolest thing I've ever seen!"

The humans come towards me with pleasure sounds on their tongues and pleasure in their eyes. I hold up my hands to ward them away, but they have no respect for boundaries whatsoever and come and *touch* me anyway.

"I am a claimed female," I shout, but they only release their pleasure-like *laughter* and thank me profusely in their own tongue. "Alright, enough!"

"Alright, folks, let's give Lisbel some space," Mercury finally has the decency to announce to the congregation.

They obey her. An older male drops his walking stick in the process and it's kicked underfoot by a youngling, this one male. I reach down and pick it up and hand it back to him. He doesn't release my hand, but rubs his soft fingers over my palm, giving it three soft pats. He smiles at me with a mouth missing two seemingly important teeth as one is near the very front and the other, in the back on the same side. The Voraxians would correct this for him. Why haven't they by now?

"Would you like to stay and pray with us, young lady?"

I balk, "I have far, far more important things to do than pray to a god I do not worship."

His grin doesn't waver. He just gives me another pat. "You name three of those things, and I'll be happy to take nox for an answer." Nox. The human male said nox.

I frown, wheels turning as I attempt desperately to think of something to get me out of this. I open my mouth and release a ragged sigh.

"My name's an old name from the old world — Robert — but folks around here call me Old Bob."

"Old Bob?" The translation comes through as *aging bob*. "And you are not offended by this?"

He laughs and before I know what's happening, he's pulling me underneath a curtain and into a wide open space. The floor is made of a fascinating substance, smooth and sleek silver that's been pocked by time, but not eroded. Now, it's just covered in intermittent markings in a language I cannot read. That, and this annoying sand.

"Can't be offended if it's family."

I stare at him in shock and place my fingers on my chest where these human females carry what look like weighty and unwieldy appendages. My chest, by contrast, is covered by thick plates that guard my vital organs. Functional, where these humans are decidedly not. Take this elderly Bob, for example. Inviting me to be his family where I could easily score his fragile skin with my claws.

"I am not your family," I protest. "I have a mate already."

He laughs. He laughs so hard I worry he'll fall to pieces. Many other members of the congregation speak and laugh amongst one another, but I don't get the impression that they're laughing *at* me. How peculiar. "Don't worry about Jaxal, now dear. I've been *mated* for eighteen long rotations. And as for family, well, family protects each other, that's what we do, and that's what you've done for us just now."

"Comets, don't misinterpret my desire to put little alphas in their place with a desire to join your family."

But he just gives me more pats on the arm, refusing to accept or acknowledge my insults just as Jaxal refuses, looks up at me with speckled green eyes, and says, "Oh Lisbel, you already are. You don't realize it yet, but soon."

# 3

## Jaxal

It's a day of rest and somebody's knocking on our door — on *my* door. I'm at the dining table, devouring a plate of something called fereranin mixed with egg substitute that actually tastes surprisingly good — all from the latest shipment the king and queen had imported. Nothing green growing yet, but the jellied, dried and hydrofrozen stuff they've brought in has been fucking divine. I shove back from the table, wiping my mouth on my napkin after I polish off the plate.

I take a step towards my front door, but I'm...brought up short.

In a wrap-dress I know for a fucking fact was made here on the colony because it's made out of the same damn brown fabric everything is, Lisbel glides to the front door, hand outstretched. I still don't fully understand what she's doing until she actually takes the doorknob and pulls on it.

It takes her two tries to get the door fully opened — it's jammed, something I've been meaning to fix. When she does, she gives her usual withering look to whoever stands on its other side.

Frozen, I'm stiff and confused as I listen.

"Lisbel, so good to see you."

"You said you would call on me. I don't see what's so good about that."

Laughter follows, several females'. "We wanted to know if you would come out with us to the market?"

Now here comes the fall. The female is as unapologetic as she is ruthless. I take a step forward, ready to apologize on her behalf, when I hear something incredible. She says, "I don't have anything to barter." *She doesn't have…wait…does that mean she's going?*

"Oh, don't worry about that. You have credits, don't you? The market stalls have started accepting Voraxian credits, too."

"Really?"

"Hexa," the females answer, giggling as they do and my female…xok…I mean *fuck*…the female living in my house she…she fucking grins.

She smiles at them.

I can only see it from the side but I don't like my response to it. *Fuck.* She's got black hair and skin that's not as dark as the darkest human on the colony, but instead of red or yellow or gold or amber undertones, her skin's more grey. It glitters like screa under the sun. Fuck she's stunning. Doesn't matter that she doesn't have tits, though I tried to tell myself it did. Doesn't matter she's got a slim waist and hips, that ass is more than enough for me to sink my cock into.

I rub my face and, when I drag my hand down, I find four females standing in my entryway staring at me. One of them's *mine.*

"So Jaxal, is it okay if we steal your mate?" Opal is looking at me with pure mischief in her gaze. I've known the woman since forever and I know she knows how I feel about aliens.

My mother was part of the Hunt. She didn't survive it. Wasn't the rape itself that killed her. It was the shame. She was a devout worshipper of the Tri-God and felt like she'd done her deity wrong. Told her a thousand times that the Tri-God would've forgiven her, but it didn't matter in the end. She drank herself to death over many rotations. Died a few rotations back.

I shouldn't have any kinda feelings about this female who made my gut clench and my cock rock hard at the first sound of her voice, but I did, and I...I still do. Looking at her standing flanked by my people, my friends — friends so good I could call them family — I can't help but shake my head and wonder what the fuck is wrong with the universe, the Tri-God, whatever the fuck you wanna call it. Because I'm fucked in the head at the sight of her.

Her eyes are dark purple. Others might not have studied them for so long. I have, but only when she's not looking.

"Jaxaaaaaal?" Trenya says in a high sing-song. She's got very light brown skin. One of the few females on the colony who does. "Anybody home?"

I bark out a laugh and brace the knuckles on my left hand on the table. "What are you all planning on doing?"

"Shop. Is that not what humans do in the market?" She's glowering at me and I'm...confused. Lisbel can be described as a stoic female. Maybe brutal, even. And I've never seen colors in her ridges except for the very first time when she was out alone on the ice and every muscle in my body had tried to hold me back from charging straight at her…and I'd failed.

But here, now, standing in between other human females all looking between us like this silence is the most entertaining thing they've ever come across, Lisbel's got a coppery color in her ridges and it's flaring quite bright. "What are you…"

She must notice my gaze because she gasps and straightens and covers her face with her hands. "I must…void!" She shouts, turning around and charging to the bathroom in the back even though she just gave me a speech a solar ago about how disgusting humans are for our need to defecate all the time.

"What the fuck are you all doing with her?" I hiss at the other women the moment she's disappeared. I advance on my friends and watch them titter, not at all in fear but in pure elation.

Celia manages to look rather surprised. She blinks at me with her large brown eyes. "We want to get to know Lisbel better. She seems cool."

"Cool?"

"And nice."

"Nice?"

I look between the three women, trying to suss out the joke, or the lie. I lean in even closer as I hear the toilet flush. I don't want her to overhear this. "No one has ever used the word *nice* to describe Lisbel. If this is some trick meant to hurt or shame her in any way, then I swear on my mother's life that I will…"

"Jaxal! Comets, no…" Celia.

"Xok, Jaxal!" Opal — and I don't miss the Voraxian word she uses.

"Jaxal, Jaxal, Jaxal…" Trenya shakes her head. She pushes her braids over her shoulder and leans in so we're speaking fully in hushed whispers now. "Did you not hear what she did?"

My muscles firm up as I anticipate horror. "What did she do?"

"Nox, not like that, Jaxal." Opal places her hand on my forearm while I fight not to murder something. "It was good. You should have more faith in her. The Tri-God certainly does." Opal smiles at me and the sheer happiness she radiates makes it hard for me to keep hold of my frown.

"Tell me." I take Opal's shoulder in my hand and give her a light, friendly squeeze.

Opal opens her mouth, but a throat clears. We look up as one unit at Lisbel standing in the center of the living room. Light filters in through the slatted windows and shimmers over her tightly crossed arms. She gives me a scalding glare before softening.

"I'm ready to leave," she says to the females. She doesn't look at me. And then, before I have a chance to discern exactly what went down and why Lisbel's getting visitors and why the fuck she's accepting them… they're off.

I'm still thinking about them as I absently wash my dishes. I break a ceramic, which fucking sucks because Celia makes these and I find them more beautiful than the efraphane plastic dishes the Voraxians brought in. As I'm cleaning up the pieces, I get another knock on my door.

Old Bob drops in with a plate of his famous root spice and cane bread — for Lisbel, for fucks sake. I try asking him what the fuck happened, but he pretends he's hard of hearing. He's not. The old bastard could hear a space ship sailing through space the next Quadrant over — worse, he knows I know it.

Two other drop-ins roll through by the time Lisbel's back — the first, Svera's parents and their other child, Ibra. The second, Mercury and her husband Nahat. All are mum about the whole damn thing, but Mercury tells me something even more bizarre — that both Pluto *and* Mars have a new hero — *Lisbel*. Somehow, that pisses me off most of all. I thought I was their hero.

The light from the suns is dimming but not yet dim by the time Lisbel returns. I'm sitting at the dining room table waiting for her, but I stand, wanting to intimidate the shit out of her. I'm the same height she is on a good day, but I don't want her to think she can fuck around with me or my community. Not gonna put up with any nefarious or dangerous shit from her and I plan to make it clear.

She comes through the door, arms laden with brown sacks. I can smell the fresh scent of cane and root bread emanating from one of them, which I pretend to hate because it means we'll be eating cane and root bread for days, but the truth of the matter is that I love cane and root bread and could eat it for rotations.

"Lisbel."

She shuts the door behind her and sets her sacks down on the floor with a thump.

"Tell me what the fuck you did last solar to have so many of my friends come by with gifts and invitations for…" She starts walking towards me, her gaze completely unfocused. I narrow mine in response and square my shoulders. "Are you even listening to me?"

She steps right up to me, coming closer to me than she's ever come before. It trips me up and I'm distracted until the moment she lifts her right wrist and swipes her clawed hand across my face. She hits me. She fuckin' hits me. The pain is an even greater shock than her proximity and I take half a step back and bring my fingers to my cheek. There's no blood, but there's a definite sting.

"What…"

The bumps above her eyebrows blaze now, turning a brittle copper. I messaged Kiki earlier about this. She'd laughed and told me, via life drive, that copper was a Voraxian and Drakesh color for *jealousy. She's jealous because of me.* "The fuck, Lisbel?"

"You touched another female and in my presence!" Her jaw is ticking, but other than that — and the color — she looks nonplussed. And she's staring at me, expecting an answer even though she hasn't even asked a question.

And she's jealous.

My shoulders ease down my spine and I tilt my head to the side. My heart is racing, but I betray only calm and indifference. "I didn't think you'd care. Or notice." I touch my cheek again, prod my tongue on the inside of it. I watch her watch it.

"Well, I did notice," she grunts, dismissing the first statement in a way that I can feel in my balls.

I lift a hand and reach to touch her face — her ridges, in particular. I haven't touched her at all. Not once. There was a moment a few solars ago when the outsides of our arms brushed and raw, unfiltered energy tingled through every single one of my pores, but then she moved into the bedroom while I sprawled out over the poofs in the living room and the energy eventually faded and I was made miserable by the fact that it happened and twice as miserable that I couldn't ask her for more. *If I had less pride, I'd've begged.*

She tenses and watches my hand until her pupil-less eyes can no longer focus on it.

"You noticed," I whisper, "and it made you jealous…"

I touch the ridge above her right eyebrow, but only for a split instant before she swats my hand away. "Do you share your xora with other females when you go out during the solar?"

I can't help it. The Voraxian word coming through the translator is a fucking gift. It makes me hard and, right now, I'm too confused and frankly, exhausted of the hatin' and the fightin' and the sexual fuckin' frustration to block out what the sound does to me. Maybe, it isn't the word at all. Maybe, it's the fact that she's starting to…I don't know…make peace with her situation, bond with my people. Make peace with me. *But have I made peace with her?*

"You want to know what I do all solar, when you won't tell me what you did on the last?"

"It doesn't concern you. Not like your cock shoved into another female's cunt. If your Xanaxana no longer calls for me, then just say so and I'll…" Her voice stutters. Her lips tremble. They're full and pretty, painted on her face in a darker grey than her skin is.

"You'll what?"

A burst of grey colors her ridges, and then an even more electric yellow sweeps the grey away. She chokes just a little bit, swallows hard. Her bottom jaw sets. Without another word, she turns from me, hair heavy as it swats my arm.

Nuh uh. Not this time.

I grab her just above the elbow and wrench her back. Her chest collides with mine. It's flat and covered by her dress. I slide my other hand around her waist and lower my head. I inhale her scent and remember what Kiki told me the last time I saw her, just after her epic battle, just after mine. I'd never been so proud of her than in that moment, but after she said what she did next, I realized I could be prouder still.

*"Hate is easy to hold onto. Letting go is hard. But if you do, you'll realize falling never felt so good. All it takes is that first slip."*

*"What slip is that?"*

*"You might not even know, but once you slip the first time, you'll slip again. And again. You can try to climb back, but that rope is slick, brother. You'll fall again and again if you do."*

*"And if I resist that very first time?"*

*She smirked at me and looked past me at Lisbel, eating at the opposite end of the long table I was. "Good luck. The Xanaxana's a slippery bitch."*

I pull. I feel Lisbel's tension and resistance as our stomachs press together. She's my height, maybe even a little taller, though I won't cede to it. Here it is, my chance to slip. I could catch tight on the rope now and drag my ass up or…

I goad her, "What would you do?"

"I'd cut off your xora in the lunar." She bites her front teeth together, but her eyes are flitting back and forth in their tipped shell. They are ringed in darkness, makeup she can't take off. She doesn't understand what I'm doing. Maybe I don't either.

"And then where would you go? Who would take you in? One of your new friends? Hm? One of the females I'd lose my dick over?"

She licks her lips. "Maybe."

"You'd live with them after?"

"I have other...*friends*." She says the word in human. I'm not sure that, in Voraxian, it exists.

I grin. "How would you know I haven't stuck my *xora* into them, too?"

"*Too?* So, you're admitting it?" She tries to rip away from me, tries to scratch me, tries to hit me, but I'm stronger than she is and hold her in my arms. I cup the back of her neck and apply pressure with the tips of my fingers hard enough to make her wince.

"Tell me it makes you jealous."

She shakes her head, stares desperately between my eyes. She thumps a fist pitifully on my chest and this time, I allow it. I'm not wearing a shirt. I always wore a shirt until I caught her looking at me without one. She'd looked away so fast when I caught her watching, I'da swore her neck might snap.

Maybe this here is the first slip, maybe it was that one or maybe, it happened even earlier. Back at the beginning. Before I even knew who she was. Back when I was just a human on this lonely little rock, wondering why I struggled so hard to find true connection with other women. Because it's not like this. It was never like this. And it never will be with anyone, because there isn't anyone else.

My voice is husky and deeper and unrecognizable to even me when I say, "Tell me..."

"You can see it already, so I don't need to use words to say…It's just…you know…you *are* my Xiveri Mate. It is your duty not to xok other females." She's scrambling.

I raise a single eyebrow. "You don't sound sure."

"I'm *not* sure! I know you don't like me — that you *hate* me. But I also know what burns in my chest. I know the weight of the Xanaxana and I'm *mad* with the idea that you xoked other females and I *hate* that you don't feel the same way."

"How do you know that I don't feel the same way?"

She stops breathing. My gaze drops to her chest. I wanna touch her so damn bad, but that's not how this is gonna work between us. Not yet.

"I…don't."

I turn my touch softer and gently sweep her hair back from her neck. I lower my face to her long, elegant throat and inhale her scent. She smells like the sands of my home and the ice of hers. An iceberg bathing in sunlight.

"Well, know this now. I do. I feel every bit as much as you do. I know that you hate me. I know that you think you deserve better than me and what I can provide…"

"I…"

"Nah. Don't lie to me. I know it like I know this ache in my body is real. Only I don't feel it in my chest," I lie, because I do. "I feel it in my *xora* and I know for a fucking fact that you wouldn't have to castrate me in the lunar, because there's no way I could take this dick to be with any other female while you're mine." And she will always be mine.

She's gone from not breathing at all to breathing like she's in a full out sprint. I try to hold, keep it together, stop myself from impaling her on my body roughly, in hate, in punishment, and in fear of slipping down this rope, too. That's not how I wanna be with any female, let alone with this one. The one some universal entity fated for me. Don't know if I ever believed in shit like that — gods or whatever — but the feeling in my body, pulsing through me like a damn tornado, can't be ignored. Won't be. Isn't. I'm listening now, but I still need to tread carefully before we slip too far, fall too fast, and end up splattered all over the ground.

"So, you…" She swallows, her body practically arched back in my grip, like she's trying to escape me. Except she's got her hand placed lightly on my shoulder. I don't know what to make of it. "So, you *don't* xok other females?"

"Nox," I tell her in Voraxian for emphasis.

"And you have no plans to?"

"Nox."

"And you haven't xoked those females in the past?"

"Nox. I fucked five females in the colony and all of 'em are happily married now."

"I want their names."

I sigh, release her and walk down the hall to the bedroom. I drop my pants and, in boxers, take a seat on the edge of the bed. She follows me, as I expected she would. It's something I like about her. Her curiosity and willingness to see things through — even if she does reject them later. Just for the sheer petulance of it. Kinda like that petulance about her, too. Makes me feel the primal male urge to punish her in the most indulgent way imaginable. *Her, bent over my knee, ass in the air, ready for a rough fuck and a good spanking.*

I shake my head, remembering that this is still Lisbel. "You crawled into the bed of my best friend's husband."

Lisbel's ridges flare a colorful swatch of yellows and I wonder if it's not something like embarrassment. *Or shame.* "I...I did not know..."

"Don't want your excuses." I really do not want her fucking excuses. "Don't want to hear shit more about what you've done to get what you thought you wanted. I'm here now. Gonna give you what you need."

"What's that?"

"Take off your clothes and get into bed."

"Verax."

"You need a good lunar's rest because the coming solar, I'm gonna show you what I'm doing all solar long and it's not fucking other women left and right. Now lie down. Sleep."

I turn off the lamp on the bedside table and douse the room in near darkness. The lunar isn't fully descended, but it will come soon enough. It never lasts long, though. The suns always chase each other back over the horizon. I roll onto my back and pull the sheet up to my hips. I make no effort not to watch her silhouette unravel itself to reveal her tall, slender form.

She isn't wearing anything at all beneath that dress and I know, when she takes it off and lies down next to me on this wide bed that suddenly feels way, way too narrow, that I'm a glutton for punishment. I wonder if she feels it...

The tension.

"Go to sleep, Lisbel," I order, my voice thick with desire.

Of course, she doesn't listen. "Jaxal?"

"Hm?"

"Do you desire me?"

"What kinda question is that?"

"Well...you haven't..."

"What? Because I don't roll over and rut you senseless, you're worried I don't *desire* you? We hate each other, remember?"

"I know that, but that's not what I was going to say," she huffs. "If you would just let me finish."

I shift on the mattress and grunt, "Then what?"

She shifts beside me, moving closer where I wanted more space. Her arm brushes against mine. Just her elbow against my elbow. She might as well be giving me head for all the good it does me. I've got a cock of steel and balls well on their way to turning blue at that little gesture, the simplest contact.

"I thought humans gave one another kiss expressions."

"What?"

"Kiss. The kiss. I thought humans do this often."

I bark out a laugh, one meaner than intended. "A kiss is shared between humans — *beings* that love one another." I don't know why I said love. Lots of humans share *the kiss* that don't. But I don't retract my statement.

"But...Xiveri is this thing you humans call *love*."

"Xiveri might be love. But it isn't *like*. I gotta like you and you gotta like me, too, before we get into *any* of the physical shit."

I roll onto my side, facing away from her before I'm tempted to do something drastic. The instant I'm settled, a foot comes against my ass and pushes. I hit the floor with a thud and by the time I stand up, Lisbel's dragged all the blankets onto her side of the mattress and is glaring up at me — I can see the light refracting off of her large, pretty eyes.

"I don't like you either," she hisses.

I laugh and slam a pillow into her face before taking it with me back into the living room. I settle down onto the poofs, throw one arm behind my head, slip my other hand underneath my boxers and stroke my dick to thoughts of Lisbel, a female I couldn't love any more than I do now, or like any less.

# 4

## Lisbel

I train only one day with the warriors before I decide definitively that I was not meant to be a warrior Xhea. I don't like the dirt, the heat, the contact. Jaxal tries to hurt me several times when sparring. He insists that he is trying to teach me how to defend myself, but I don't believe a word out of his lovely, lying lips. They are so very lovely, especially when he's being severe…

I won't think of it. If he doesn't want to kiss me, I'm not going to force him. I don't know why I'm so determined to partake in such a clumsy, foolish human tradition anyway.

So, I spend the next three solars cooped up in my home. I occasionally help Mercury and  the other members of the Tri-God congregation with small, mundane tasks. Finally, by the sixth day of isolation I…I do something odd.

I approach their group and *ask* to help them with something.

They take me up on my offer immediately and I find myself strangely delighted to partake in their strange tasks, which range from needling clothing to creating food products like *butt-her*, whose content I cannot and don't want to fathom.

I do this for six solars straight during which time Jaxal and I grow…closer? Closer to tolerating one another, at least. We don't share the same bed, though I wish I hadn't kicked him out because he doesn't fight me to try sleeping at my side a second time and, despite the fact that I don't *like* him, I *would* like to try the kissing action with him and maybe even…more. I *ache* in embarrassing ways…ways I never ached for the Okkari, or any male. Not even close.

I know he is less affected than I because he makes no further attempt to touch me and I absolutely will not be the first to approach him with my needs. It is *his* duty as my Xiveri to know these things. Naturally.

Naturally…

And this is why, some lunars later, when I come home from helping Mercury and Celia and other humans bake fine ceramics in an oven in the earth, covered in dust, I am confused to find Jaxal missing from the lounge area…and the cooking pit…and he isn't in the void room…

"I'm in the bedroom. Lisbel, come here."

Curious, but slightly alarmed by the tone of his voice, I approach the opening to my bedroom — his bedroom…*our* bedroom? I peek my head around the corner to see Jaxal sitting on the edge of the bed facing me. He's got his hands on his knees and he's bare-chested because he pretends he doesn't even own a tunic even though I've seen countless hung up in his closet. I wonder if he notices me noticing him. Probably not. These humans rarely ever notice the details.

He doesn't have any plates, which I find rather *erotic*. So different than what I know. And the hair… Voraxians don't have hair on their bodies and *my stars*… His pants are unlaced at the top and fanned open so I can see a spread of thick, coarse hair descending into his pants.

My mouth waters.

"Hexa?"

His ensuing growl makes me flinch. It also makes my nipples tighten. "Come here." I enter the room. "Close the door behind you." I close the door and glance around.

The windows are open and the light outside is dimming, but not yet black. There are candles on the dressers to my right and the small desk to my left. I wonder why the candles are lit and not the lamps. Does he know how much I enjoy candles? We don't have candles on Nobu. They don't stay lit in the cold. And these look particularly special. Pinks and blues, greens and purples. They are lumpy and ill formed, like each one was handcrafted by some artisan here on this world.

"I like the cand…"

He cuts me off. "I'm going to need you to take off your skirt and lie down over my lap." He pats his inner leg twice in a way that makes my pussy lips pulse and my inner thighs tremble.

"Verax."

"No. No verax. You're in severe need of punishment."

*"Punishment?"*

"And reward."

"Reward?"

"You hard of hearing or do you simply enjoy the sound of my voice?" The corner of his mouth twitches, which makes me feel a universe better. This severity isn't like him and I hate to admit that I'm both a little afraid and wholly aroused by it.

"I…"

"You'll get the reward after the punishment. But the punishment comes first. Come now, lie down across my lap on the bed."

I take a step forward automatically before I catch myself, remember who I am and what is going on between us. "You cannot talk to me like this."

"Your punishment just got worse, Lisbel." I do like how he says my name, the way he hisses the S so sibilantly.

I take another half step before retreating.

He stands and comes towards me and I back up before finding resolve. I plant my feet firmly and hold my ground which, in retrospect, was a rather poor choice. He slides his fingers underneath the waist of my skirt and frees the ties. It pools at my feet before I can catch it and before I know what's happening or can think of what I need to do to stop this, he's got his arms snugly fixed around my waist and his lips are plunging towards my mouth. I worry about such an attack because the gesture is so alien to me until I remember that it *is* alien. And it's also what I asked for.

With his warm, soft mouth on mine, he delivers the kiss to me.

His lips mold to fit mine, upper lip above, lower lip between my own. His tongue strokes my upper lip and his teeth nibble on it in a rough way that sends a little pain careening through me like the wind, while a warm gale of pleasure swirls up from my toes. All six of my grey toes curl into my sandals and I find myself lifting up onto the balls of my feet, attempting to chase him as he pulls away again.

My head is spinning when he slides his hand from my waist to my hip to my thigh. His knuckles brush over my mound and I make an embarrassing sound as I pray to Xana herself for him to continue to touch me just a little bit more…

Like a clever drunk, I manage to right myself when he tows me forward but, before I can decipher what he's up to or stop it, he's already sitting on the bed and I'm lying spread out on top of him. My belly presses into the tops of his thighs while my breasts and knees press firmly into the mattress. I try to lift myself up, but he snags both of my wrists in one of his five-fingered hands and traps them against my lower back. His other hand strokes the curve of my ass in a way that I can't interpret. Is it a threat? Why does it feel like a threat?

And then he smacks me *hard* right on the fleshy, sensitive part of my leg where my thigh and my ass meet. He does it again three more times in quick succession while I mutter angry curses and start thrashing. He uses force to hold me down and I whimper, a little scared.

"I don't like this," I say, forcing back a sniffle.

He stops immediately and brushes my hair over my ear. I can't see his face, but I can feel his soft movements over my sensitive skin as he passes his fingers in lazy caresses over the bruises he just created. "You're not supposed to like it. It's your punishment."

"For what?"

"For standing up to four barbaric Voraxians and putting yourself in danger. They could have attacked or killed you and, under Voraxian law, they'd likely get off.

Your *laws* don't seem to apply here. They haven't for generations."

Shock entirely removes me from this situation and takes me back to that one. I hadn't considered the possibility that those males might try to hurt me. On Nobu, it would be unheard of for a male to harm a female and yet…I can't forget all the horrors that happened to the females here, the human females. And those Voraxian males, they view me now as one of the humans.

I swallow hard and…and oh stars…water comes to my eyes. Tears. The humans call these tears. I bury my face in the mattress and the soft blankets that cover it. "I didn't think of that," I mewl.

"You're mine to protect, my Xiveri. If they'd taken you from me, just like they took my mother from me, I'd have had to kill them." Wait. Verax. They took his mother from him? "As much as I'd like to rip off their plates, I promised Kiki I'd be good. I don't like to lie to my friends. And that you didn't tell me means you lied to me. Are we not even friends, Lisbel?"

"We…we are friends," I sniffle pitifully.

"I don't think we are." He slaps me again and I'm not prepared for it.

I squeal, "We are!"

"Shh. Stop lying."

"I'm not."

Another swat. "You are." He leans to the side, planting one elbow on the bed so he can reach my face with his own. He pulls my face to the side when I try to recoil from him and hide in the sheets. He tucks my hair behind my ear. "How can we be friends if you don't even like me?"

"I do like you a little."

He grins and it's a ravenous thing. "That might be the first truth you've told." He leans in towards me and kisses just the tip of my nose, then brushes his lips between my eyes. He lingers over my ridges, sweeping one with his impossibly soft, yet firm lips before laving the other with the tip of his tongue.

When he pulls back, I can see lights brightly reflected off of his face, but he isn't staring at my ridges. He's staring into my eyes, *seeing* me beyond my born name, beyond my crimes, beyond my hard shell and my even harder interior.

I won't retreat from it because I've never retreated from anything even though a small, frightened part of me wants to. "Maybe."

He snorts and the unattractive sound sends heat through my lower half. "A second truth. Do you think you deserve a reward for that?"

"You said at the beginning of this that I was already getting a reward."

"Cheeky little fighter."

"Fighter? I'm hardly a fighter."

"That's not what the others told me about your interaction with the Voraxians. They said you spoke down to the Voraxians as if you were a giant and them, two feet tall. You stood in defense of my people and my family, even at risk to yourself. The risk is why I'm punishing you. But what you did for the Tri-God congregation deserves something else. Do you want your reward?"

I nod before I can catch myself and try to play it coy.

He doesn't laugh at me though. His gaze just travels down my face to my throat. He strokes the backs of his knuckles over the plates covering my chest. His thumb is rough when it presses down on my nipple. "Do you have sensitivity here?"

"Not much." But some. Every place his skin makes contact with mine seems to fuel a deep and ardent desire.

"Hm." His head tilts to the side and he slides one hand behind my back and in an artful movement, switches our positions.

He pulls me off of him, onto my back on the mattress and maneuvers himself onto his side. He lines my body with his and rumbles deep in his chest. He appraises me with his gaze and I struggle to understand his response. It makes me…uneasy.

"Why do you look at me like this?"

"Like what?"

"I'm not sure…"

"Like you're fucking beautiful? Beautiful enough to swallow whole." His nostrils flare as he exhales in a rush. "But first, I need to find where you are sensitive. Give me a sign when I get close." He bends his head and kisses my cheek.

"What sign," I say, my voice cracking, "should I give you?"

He kisses my bottom lip, lightly at first, before he sucks it into his mouth. Sensation ripples down my back and down the backs of my legs all the way to my heels. I dig them into the mattress, fighting against the embarrassing sounds threatening to slip out of my mouth. I lose hold of the reins I once held and the sound just flutters out, like a desperate wail — mainly because it is. He pulls back but I want more of this thing these humans call *kiss*.

"That's a good enough sign for me." He smiles and his teeth are white, flawlessly so. I lurch up and grab him by the back of the neck, bring him back down to my mouth and try to replicate the movements of his.

Our teeth clack together and Jaxal laughs between us. "Easy," he says and he slows the pecking and the puckering and the laving and the easy rhythm with which he kisses me until I'm able to follow.

"Don't tease me." I rake my claws down his chest, applying pressure, but not enough to break his skin that's so much smoother and thinner than the rough plates I have to protect me. I wonder if he…finds my plates unsightly. I don't get the chance to ask. Before I can think beyond my irritation at being toyed with, he grabs my offending wrist and bites on the pulse pounding through it until I moan even louder.

He laughs. "You're mine to tease how I please, now hold still."

He moves down my body, tasting every curve, every crest. I understand my earlier punishment now and I'm certain that I'll become a glutton for it, if it's followed each time by a reward like this. I don't make any effort not to move, but undulate and writhe and twist as his teeth and fingers and tongue move over my body freely, as if I'm owned. As if I'm his.

My moans are louder at the pressure he applies to my ears — behind them, especially — and at my inner elbow crease, my ribs below the thick plates on my chest, and then my legs…xok, what's he doing with my legs?

"What…what…what are you doing down there?" I gasp, unable to catch my breath as he works his way down my plated left outer leg and then back up my plate-less inner left thigh. He makes it to the crease where my thigh meets my pelvis and when he presses his kiss directly onto my mound, I just about die.

"Jaxal!" I scream his name and jerk up onto my elbows. Looking at him in the candlelight, I can see everything — every rugged line of his face, his shadow of a beard, his right cheek's dimple. I'm certain I've never seen anyone so beautiful. "What…"

He winks as I watch him over my body. "Made you moan, gasp, scream my name, but I think I can do better." My chest is heaving, my twelve toes gripping at the air just as my twelve fingers grip at the sheets.

He moves back in, but I jerk until the top of my head collides with the wall behind our bed. "I'm certain you can do no more. I'm already on *fire*."

"Hexa," he says, and I worship the sound of his voice in the Voraxian tongue. "But sometimes, fires cause explosions."

He dives between my thighs and holds my hips down for good measure. My mound is smooth and hairless, but sensitive. I can feel every scrape and brush of his beard against it. And when he sticks his tongue inside and reaches the most sensitive part of me, I ascend to the stars.

"Comets!" The Xanaxana rears its head and decimates me with its claws.

The first effects of it that came over me back on the harsh icy plains of Nobu are nothing compared to this total inundation. Obliteration.

His tongue strokes the sensitive place inside of me and I rise…and rise…and rise. I reach down and grab hold of his hair, fisting the thick, coiled strands with all twelve of my fingers. I pull him closer into me and can feel how he laughs against my parted folds even without missing a beat.

"Oh…oh! There…please…" And then I reach out and brush my fingers across the cosmos that I came from, that birthed me and then delivered me here into the arms of a male who has never seen them as I have seen them. But it doesn't matter at all.

I wanted to be queen to a king. What I got instead? The most sublime fall. And as I come down I realize that where I've landed is a pretty perfect place to be.

I'm gasping when I come crashing down onto the bed in a thunderous and angry violence. I'm shouting Jaxal's name, pulling on his hair, trying to wrestle him up my body just so I can slap him across the face.

"What the fuck was that for?"

"You are too proficient in this! Who else have you practiced this on?"

Jaxal manages to wrangle my hands down onto the bed on either side of my face. He straddles my waist, so I'm completely at his mercy as he stares down at me with round eyes and a wild grin. "You're a fucking nutjob," he shouts, and then hisses when I buck up against his hips. "And I really fucking like it."

He maneuvers himself so that his pelvis is in line with mine. My legs spread around his hips and I hook my ankles behind his lower back, wanting him closer, wanting to claim him as his bloated erection prods my core.

As it does, I debase myself and whisper, "Do you… like me, too?"

His gaze meets mine. He settles onto his forearms so that his chest is pressed against mine. I'm pinned between him and our mattress and I have never felt so cared for, or so cherished, or so...*wanted*. He winks at me. "Just a little bit." And then he presses his hips forward and I feel the bulge of his erection press at my opening...just before he slides into me all the way up to the hilt.

I am overwhelmed by the sensation and I come for him instantly. Pleasure centers line my  channel and his cock is thick and hard enough to hit all of them with every thrust.

"Fucking stars," I think I hear him hiss above me. "Are you coming again?"

"Hexa..." My eyes roll back. "And I will not stop..."

And I don't stop. I come endlessly as he slams into me over and over, taking me to the cosmos and back. He pumps into me until my bones turn to soup and my brain, mush. Even as I become near comatose, he simply laughs at me, turns me over onto my belly, and spanks me hard enough to bring me back.

I thrust backwards into his hips and when he releases an almost beastlike growl, I do it again. "Fuck, yes. That's it. Come on, baby." He gives me these strange words of encouragement and I find that I like them so much, they cause renewed rushes of energy to flood my bones. My eyes roll back and what feels like pure magic shimmers around us.

I worry he can't feel it, but then, in the midst of the cacophony, he says, "What is this, Lisbel?"

*Xanaxana*, I mean to answer. "I love you, Jaxal," is what I say instead.

He roars out his release and I feel as his cock bucks in my tight channel, lubricating it more than it was already wetted by his wonderful mouth. He collapses over me and bites down on my shoulder, making me worry that he may be some sort of manerak barbarian — a creature that is fabled to live outside of the known quadrants and features in ancient Voraxian storybooks — intent on gobbling me up. But his teeth are blunt and all they cause is pleasure.

"I love you too, Lisbel." I come undone as he falls on top of me and takes me to our bed. His breath is hot and heavy against my ear and I'm already half asleep when he says, "I might even like you."

# 5

## Jaxal

It's the middle of the lunar and we should be asleep, but we're not. We're both feverish, too busy sating ourselves on each other, unable to quench this unending thirst. It's been like this for four solars and each one of them is pure fucking ecstasy. I'm wrecked, endlessly.

And what's more…I don't know…*meaningful* than the way we fuck is what happens after. She kisses me nonstop. It's cute. She fumbles, clearly not having done this before, and that's even cuter. Her teeth against my neck nip in a way I'd consider playful if she were human, but her fangs are too rough. I jerk away from her.

"Ow, that hurts." I laugh.

I can't see her. It's too dark. I know she likes to use the candles, but they blew out some time back. Plus, we have to use them sparingly considering how hard they are to make, how rare they're becoming as we adopt more and more Voraxian technology, and how much I had to barter for these few. I'd do it again though. There's a lot I'd do for her that I never thought I'd ever do for one of these beings. Or for anyone.

"Jaxal?"

I smile into the dark and lazily comb my fingers through her hair. It drops heavier than human hair and fascinates me. So much of her fascinates me. "I'm here."

"I know that." I can practically feel her rolling her eyes even though it's not something Voraxians do — or if they do it, I can't tell because they don't have pupils or irises. She huffs and repositions her face higher up on my chest. I can feel her cool breath on the underside of my chin and I wonder how well she can see in the dark. I don't need her looking straight up my nose at all my nose hairs. She doesn't have any hair on her body at all. Thought it would bother me, not seeing any pubic hair on her but turns out…it doesn't.

"Your mother was a female killed in the Hunt?"

I feel like I should have tensed in the exact moment I realize I don't. I don't react at all. I exhale and kiss the top of Lisbel's head, pulling her close. "Not exactly. She was raped in the Hunt, but she killed herself after. It was the shame of it. The horror. But she was also sick. She was for a long time after my dad died."

"What happened to him?"

"He was a lot older than she was and a hunter. He was hunting well past his prime and got caught in a screa landslide. My mom didn't cope well…or, I guess, she coped well with alcohol."

"She missed him."

I sigh, "Yes."

"He was her Xiveri?"

"No doubt about it. He loved her when he shouldn't have."

"What does that mean?"

"He loved her before she was of age and the moment she passed her seventh rotation, he was bent on courting her."

I can feel Lisbel's smile under my fingertips as they roam her face. I can almost see my mom's smile when I close my eyes and stare up at the ceiling. I can almost see both of my parents. "That sounds very much like Raku and the Rakukanna. He knew she was his Xiveri before she had seen her seventh rotation. I have heard the rumors of his reaction when he realized he could not take her with him — that to take her would be a disgrace."

I smirk, "I've heard them, too. It's a miracle our moon's still in existence."

Lisbel laughs. It's a light, wholly feminine sound and makes me worry that I have an entirely different female in my arms — one that actually might be *nice*. I don't want nice, though. I want Lisbel and all her thorny parts.

She says, "You lost both your sires so young."

"I don't feel that young." I chuckle.

"I asked your friends. Perhaps I am like your father, too. I am a full two rotations older than you are."

"Are you?" I exhale, eyes closed, so fucking relaxed, even as we talk about ghosts.

"It doesn't bother you?"

"Why would it bother me?"

"You're xoking an old maid."

I grin and rotate until I'm hovering over her. I laugh down into her mouth and inhale her scent. *That iceberg is melting right quick.* "You move good for an old lady."

She hits me and I block, expecting it. She's hit me a thousand times since that very first time. I should be more pissed but I like punishing her for it far, far too much to tell her to quit.

I lean in and kiss her deeply, guiding her tongue with mine, moving it the way I want to move it. I break the kiss and reposition myself between her legs, fully intent on fucking her again *and again and again* but she places her hand on my chest right over my heart.

"Jaxal?"

Something in her tone makes me pause. "Yeah?"

"I'm sorry for what my kind has done to yours."

Her words *move* me. A power that I know fully well to be the Xanaxana shifts, like a large rock rolling in my chest. It uncovers a great chasm. And what am I doing? I'm just a lonely idiot trying to hold onto the tattered end of a rope to avoid the fall. But I'm already six feet under.

Choking back emotion, I tell her, "I'm sorry for what your kind has done to you."

"I'm not." She shudders when she inhales and I slide off of her and pull her close. I pull the blanket over us and wrap every inch of my body and being around her. "I deserve my fate."

"Is it really so bad a fate?"

"Nox…nox, that isn't what I meant." She shifts to wrap her arms around me, holding me back just as fiercely. "I meant that I deserved to be exiled from my home world. I deserved that fate, but I don't know yet if I deserve…" Her voice fades.

I give her a nudge. "What?"

"I'm sorry about your mother," she deflects.

"I know that. I can sense it and I appreciate you saying that." More than she can ever know. "But I want to know what you were going to say. What fate don't you deserve?"

And in the tiniest, littlest, nearly inaudible voice, she says, "You."

# 6

## Lisbel

It's my twelfth solar helping the humans at the dirty pile of space rubble and I have to admit, I find the site rather charming. Perhaps, just the creatures in it. Either way, I feel oddly…content. Perhaps, it isn't so odd.

I've just come from dumping excess oil from the disgusting *butt-her* in a vat away from their holy wreck — because of the smell, which is among the foulest substances in the known Quadrants — when, of all this planet's strange and bizarre creatures, I'm approached by Pluto. And the little creature is sobbing.

"Please! Please come, Lisbel."

She grabs my hand and starts to pull me off somewhere. Where to? I have no idea, but I plod along after her, confused. "Where is your mother?"

"I couldn't…couldn't find her!" She screams, the sobs so violent, she can barely walk.

"Calm yourself, little kitling. Look at me. Tell me what's wrong?"

But she just wails and, as she leads me around the outskirts of the human villages, I realize we're heading towards the new constructions being built on the mountain. On the other side of the hill the Droherion protection dome shimmers in the bright solar light, yet as we draw nearer to it, I grow uneasy.

"Pluto, we should find your mother."

"No…no time," she squeals, face covered in liquids that I wouldn't go near without a space suit on. She needs her mother to fix…whatever is happening here.

"Pluto, we draw far too close to the dome's perimeter. There are monsters here."

"Hex…hex…hexa…" She belts out a sob and drags me around the base of the hill, past dozens of Voraxian and human builders lugging materials back and forth, staring at us with shock and confusion as we pass.

And then finally, the sounds of chaos fade, and I realize we're on the shadowy side of the hill, just out of sight of the builders diligently doing their jobs, and away from the prying eyes of the other humans in the settlement…and it's here that I see what Pluto means. There *are* monsters here — three of the four Voraxians who I stood up to before now have Pluto's brother Mars in their grip.

My feet thunder over the packed red sand just as the shortest of them pushes Mars to the ground.

I grab Pluto by the arm and drop my face so that I can stare directly into her eyes. "Go find Jaxal and then go find your mother. In that order, do you understand?"

She nods frantically, but I shake my head, grab either side of her face and use four of my twelve fingers to wipe away the awful liquids. "You are stronger than this. Be brave. Now run."

She flies. Well, she totters a bit, but she still manages to disappear into the human colony where I hope she has the sense to go find Jaxal with the other hunters. Even though they aren't needed to hunt so often anymore, they still train as warriors…in case. There is still so little trust between our species.

Between Jaxal and I.

We share our bed every lunar and we still struggle in the daylight.

And it's a beautiful struggle. Magical, really.

What did that old man say once? *We fight for each other because we're family…*

Mars sits on his bottom on the ground, a wooden stick in his hand that looks like a shorter version of the practice staffs Jaxal keeps around our house. Tears streak through the red dirt stuck to his dark brown skin and clothes. I'm within shouting distance now of the cluster and shout I do, fully aware that this will most definitely earn me a severe punishment later.

I look forward to it.

"You there! xub'imbecile!" The male in question doesn't turn, but one of his cronies taps him on the arm. Together, the group pivots to face me and, when I'm close enough, surrounds me.

I throw my hands onto my hips, toss my shoulders back and shriek, "Goblin, you've disgraced yourself. Tormenting a kit because you can't find a real adversary? Goblin, Goblin, Goblin, that's low. Even for you."

"What does she keep calling you?" One of them whispers to the other. "Gob…Gob…"

"That's his title isn't it?" I snap. "xub'Gogo or Goblin or Goosebloop or something nonsensical?"

"Nonsensical?" He roars, turning away from the kit and rushing towards me until we're separated by an arm's length. A very short arm. "We build civilizations and you dare call us nonsensical…or interfere with our duty to punish this kit! This kit and the smaller one were tampering with our equipment."

"It's a kit, you imbecile!"

"It's a human…" While he's rambling, I glance at Mars on the ground and make a small gesture with my fingers. The kit is cleverer than I gave human kits credit for being — he does not waste his opportunity. He runs…only for Gorgon to step on his foot — with *force*.

I scream bloody murder, "He's a *kit!* They are both kits — *Voraxian* kits, by the edict of the Raku and the Rakukanna." My voice is incredulous and I do not restrain the colors in my ridges, not this time. They are awash with red rage and yellow with shame on his behalf and mine. "You shame every creature of Voraxia with your display, *including me* and I will not be shamed by the likes of a brute only half as intelligent as the rocks he lugs from one side of the Quadrant to another!"

I don't see it coming. He flings his fist towards my face and I crumple instantly. I hit the packed sand and I just lay there for a moment, wondering what in the stars has happened. I stare up at the blinding light of the bright white sky and then I twist my neck so that I can look out at the packed red sands. I see Mars watching me with a quivering lower lip, but the moment our eyes lock, determination sets in his. He lifts his staff and swats the back of Goblin's calf. Goblin turns on the boy and lifts his own hand in response.

"Don't you xoking dare!" I scream while the first dredges of pain filter through me. Spots of bright purple and blue colors dance radiantly in my sight, blocking it, but I still heave myself up into a sitting position and score Gorgon's leg with my claws.

He hisses and as he turns his attentions back to me, he meets my ire…and a rock. It clunks him in the center of his forehead and we all look back in a choreographed movement. I twist and it feels horrible, the pain bubbling up in my forehead. *Is this what it feels like to get hit? Xoking seasons, why does anyone bother fighting anyone ever? This is awful.* It also fills me with keen awareness that Jaxal, for all his efforts to train me, never hurt me even though he could have, even on accident. But he never did. Because he is a controlled, kind male and this Goblin, fellow, is merely an abominable thing.

I reach up and cup my cheek while my vision slowly clears…to the sight of Old Bob with his walking stick and a ring of humans standing behind him. Ten, twelve, perhaps, or maybe only six and I'm still seeing double. Either way, many members of this religious congregation I've been working with are present. The priestess Corane, Ibra, Mahmoud, and Heba. Many others whose names I pretend not to know, but do. Trenya. Celia is the one holding a rock. Beside her is Opal. She's holding two.

"You alright there Lisbel? Mars?" Old Bob is looking at me, his eyes full of so much emotion. I struggle to read human emotions, but this time, it is clear — concern. I know it well. I've seen it before. He's concerned for me, for us. They all are.

"Of course, I'm not, Old Bob. How could I ever be? I was just hit in the face by a moron! This…this buffoon just hit me!"

Mars releases a small sob he tries to muffle, but can't. At the same time, Mercury runs up to us from the south, screaming, "Mars!" She's gripping Pluto's hand and practically dragging the sobbing kit along behind her.

The scene breaks my heart and when the distraction of Mercury and Pluto pulls the xub'Goon's attention away from me to them, I score his leg a second time — two more times — in rapid succession.

He turns, copper blood dripping down his leg. "Lisbel, you're a filthy xoking disgrace consorting with these creatures!"

"At least my name isn't xub'Goo!"

"My name *isn't* g-g-g…" He stutters.

I don't let him finish. "*Who xoking cares?* You're a male who spends his time bullying kits and exiled females! You are worthless and no one in this Quadrant or the next gives a *fuck* about you!"

He raises his arm again and his *friend* behind him has sense enough to try to warn him away from what he's doing.

I don't close my eyes, fully intent on meeting his gaze as he brings his fist down only…it never falls. A flash of stalyx and *then* his arm falls…but when it does, it isn't connected to the rest of him. It tips from its perch at the root of his shoulder and bounces on the ground towards Mars in a fountain of copper and cries.

Mars panics and scrambles back, foot still thankfully intact. He reaches his mother who scoops him up and the family moves together as one tightly embracing unit, back past the soldier who's just lopped off Goblin's arm — the only soldier it could be, *mine* — and into the fold of humans. When Old Bob gestures for me to do the same, I comply happily and hastily.

Goblin screams in pain and I edge on my bottom over the rough sand, backing away from him while the Voraxians react to the mutilation of one of their own. They draw their stalyx swords from their belts and begin brandishing them. One of them shouts at Jaxal, "You have just committed the ultimate crime and we are fully within our rights to defend ourselves with lethal force."

Though he isn't speaking to me, his *gall* has me shaking with rage. I stop moving long enough to point up at him, hands and voice both heavy with accusation. I scream, "You come to *our* territory, corner one of *our* kits on the basis of his breeding alone and then *dare* claim self-defense? The *audacity*. *Who* are *you*? Are you even born of the same stardust we are? Or are you simply *cowards*? The Raku and his Rakukanna will have your plates for this!"

"Nox, Lisbel," comes Jaxal's low voice and it is perhaps the only thing that could have torn my attention away from Goosepoop right now.

I've never heard him speak like this.

I look to the right and see him bare-chested — *yum* — holding a bloody sword. He's dragging the entire force of the human fighting contingent with him, Nahat among them. Among the soldiers, he is the only one who advances towards us, though. He charges his family, wrapping his arms around the embracing trio. They hug him right back and my heart catches at the sight of them. But I'm also concerned...Why do the rest hang back? Why don't they come to our aid?

And then I finally lift my gaze to really look at Jaxal's face.

He's looking at me, not at his adversaries — the two standing Voraxians or the one on the ground lamenting the loss of his left arm. My mouth dries. He says, "The Raku and the Rakukanna can stay in Illyria for all I care. *I* will have their plates for this. For you."

One of the Voraxian males steps around xub'Idiot's body. His *friend* steps up beside him, points his sword at Jaxal and says, "You are the human who couldn't best the xcleranx at the trial for your mate. You stand no chance against us."

"I am." The first male lunges before Jaxal's feet are even set. I scream, but Jaxal easily deflects with a single bat of his blade. "But that was on the ice." He lunges and scores the Voraxian across both of his chest plates. "Let's see how you do on the sand."

He spins and pulls both fighters away from me, away from all of us. He leads them towards the shimmery dome that keeps the harshest elements out — and the monsters.

"Oh my stars!" I shriek, fingers flailing as I point to the barrier and the creatures lurking beyond them. "Khrui!"

A pod of at least six khrui monsters sniffs right at the edge of the Droherion dome. They stand over a dozen feet long, including their seven arms. With grey bodies covered in fur, they are menacing, terrible carnivores that shred their prey apart with claws before devouring them with sharp, serrated teeth.

Though they can't come past the barrier, if Jaxal takes one step out, they could — and will — grab him and eat him. "Jaxal, there are khrui!"

"He knows," one of the human hunters shouts to me.

"Well, why aren't you helping him, you…you!?" I can't find an insult, I'm too frazzled. Too scared out of my xoking wits. And I realize that this is *exactly* how the Okkari must have felt when I betrayed the Xhea and sent her out into Nobu's ice plains to face the hevarr — and between the hevarr and the khrui, the hevarr is the far more frightening beast. I worry my lower lip between my teeth as I realize just how badly I've *wronged* the Okkari. I don't think I realized how much until now.

The hunter says, "Because Jaxal told us not to."

"He's doing this for you," another adds.

"I didn't ask him to!"

"But that's what family does," says a whispered voice at my back. I look up and see Old Bob standing there. He offers me a smile, I think just to distract me or himself, because I can hear the sounds of struggle behind me and I'm terrified. "We protect each other."

He offers me his hand and I take it and rise to stand beside him.

I hear Jaxal's pain and feel it flutter through my whole body. He's got blood on his chest that wasn't there before. I close my eyes, pray to Xana herself — and then to whatever Tri-God watches over these surviving humans, too.

Jaxal and the idiots are right at the barrier now. The sun glints off of its surface like some rare and deadly gem. Jaxal spins, deflects the blade of one Voraxian, and then stabs the other through the gut. He drags his weapon horizontally across the Voraxian's stomach and I watch as plates peel away from flesh and flesh separates over muscle and bone and intestines and other horrifying things come tumbling out onto the packed red sands.

The other Voraxian comes charging forward, but Jaxal leans back and kicks him in the center of the chest and then moves like a propeller, wielding his blade above his head. He cuts the head from the other Voraxian before I realize the stroke has fallen. I'm about to cheer with the other humans who've gone absolutely mental until I realize that the Voraxian, Goblin, is still very much alive and right now, trying to claw his way towards me and Old Bob.

I squeak in panic as his remaining hand brushes the sole of my sandal. And then comes a decisive swat of a cane on his wrist.

He hisses and tries to grab for it, but a shadow falls over us. Goblin looks up. I look up. Jaxal looks down. He stabs his blade into the sands, spearing it straight through Golog's free and flailing arm. Then he comes to me, ignoring Gooble's shouts of pain and rage as he bucks on the ground in an attempt to free himself, but can't.

"Jaxal, I..."

Jaxal's gaze moves over my face. His hands move around my neck. He tips my face to the left and to the right. "Where did he hurt you?"

"I..." I'm overwhelmed. The pressure of his fingertips on my chin as he tilts my face up towards the sun. The squint of his eyes against it. The hard line of his jaw. His beautiful earthen skin. He was born of sunlight. He was born to belong to me and me to him.

Jaxal's face darkens and his teeth press into his lips, which thin into a single line. "He hit you?"

I nod.

"How bad does it hurt?"

"Terribly. I've never experienced anything so dreadful."

He inhales. The corner of his mouth twitches before he glances over my shoulder. "And Mars?"

"Stepped on his foot. He might have broken it, the beast."

"Would have," Old Bob adds, "had Lisbel not gotten there first. I tried to get there sooner, but I was too slow. Didn't stop me from hearing every word Lisbel said to the Voraxian though. She fought admirably for the boy."

"I believe it," Jaxal exhales. He looks deep into my gaze and I tumble into his. "She's a warrior queen." He nods at me once before I can respond, turns, and hacks off both of Goo's feet.

The humans are silent now as he drags the corpse to the edge of the barrier and then…steps through it. He tosses Goblin's body out of the Droherion dome quickly, then comes back inside, leaving the screaming Voraxian *alive* as the khrui begin to feast.

I…who am of the harshest planet, Nobu…have a *difficult* time watching the khrui as they remove his limbs, his intestines, his plates…the khrui kits feast on his ears. I think one of them has a bone in one of its seven hands and is using it as a toy. They make sounds of absolute delight over the corpse.

I close my eyes and blot out the sound as a new feeling builds in my entire body and swells in my swelling eyelid. I open the other as I sense Jaxal in front of me. He takes either side of my face in his strong hands and stares into my good eye.

I say breathily, "You didn't have to do that for me."

"I know." His voice is rough.

"I never thought less of you for not winning on Nobu."

"I know."

"You're a king to me, Jaxal."

"And you're a warrior to me, Lisbel." He smiles with one edge of his mouth and everything in the entire cosmos is right again. The shocked sound — half-laugh, half-sob — that I'd been withholding tumbles out.

"And I do like you, Jaxal."

He laughs outright at that and shakes his head, as if he didn't just cover the ground in the blood of creatures I should have felt some sympathy towards and kinship with. He slides his arms beneath me and lifts me up, like I'm some small, fragile thing even though I'm one of the tallest, toughest beings on this little, inconsequential moon.

My mate's home.

Mine, too.

"I like you, too, Lisbel."

"You don't understand." I lay my head on his chest and listen to the beating of his heart. "I like you more than anything."

# 7

## Jaxal

My trial is short, the verdict swiftly delivered. Not the way it woulda been done by Mathilda and the Council, but the Voraxian way worked out for me much better.

In many ways, they're still a primitive, barbaric species that hold special reverence for strength — and prizes Xiveri above all else. I bested three Voraxians in combat after their assault on Mars and Lisbel. According to the Voraxians, my trial was served in that instant and their punishment, just as swiftly met.

Not so into punishments though. I'm more about rewards.

"You're sure this is a reward?" I tease.

She swats my thigh, making me flinch because I wouldn't put it past Lisbel to slap my dick. "This is a reward. I haven't done it before, but I asked your other *girlfriends* for many tips."

I growl and sit up, slide my fingers into her hair and yank her towards me. Our lips collide and bolts of fire shoot through my groin, demanding that I rut her. "So reward me, then."

I haul her up against my body and she gasps as I pull her directly onto my cock. I've licked her relentlessly all daybreak, which more than makes up for the fact that her orgasm produces less wetness than a human woman's would. Also just gives me an extra excuse to come inside her over and over again. Already used this pretty pussy twice this morning. I fucking love how responsive she is.

"You didn't…let me…try…"

"I know what you wanted to try and I'm gonna shove my cock down your throat and let you lick it clean for me right after this. Just need you again. Need to feel your heart…beating against me." I don't know if she can understand a word I'm fucking saying. I'm so lost. So damn lost in the rough way her chest rubs against mine and the wild way her fingers move over every inch of me. Her six toes dig into the mattress and her thighs squeeze me within an inch of my life, telling me that I'd gladly give mine up for hers a thousand times over.

"How did it end up like this?" I say, though I didn't mean to say the words out loud.

"I don't know."

I break our next kiss roughly as she orgasms all over my cock, squeezing it in her narrow shaft like she wants to snap it clean off. I palm her cheek, careful of the bruising. I tuck her hair behind her ear, relishing in its softness. "How did I get so lucky?"

"Luck had nothing to do with it…" She pants, eyes unfocused, ridges dazzling in their color spectrum. "It was Xana…and Xaneru."

"Thank xok for them." I kiss the tip of her nose as I jack my hips up and release into her in waves of euphoria.

And in the midst of it all, I feel her pull my earlobe into her mouth, teasing it with her fangs. She whispers, "Every solar, I thank them for you."

I grin, my eyes closed, my arms wrapped around my female in our bed in our home on our small little moon, among the smallest in the cosmos and I feel it finally arrive, finally settle. The Xanaxana in all its infinite mass is home. I've fallen, but I'm not done yet because I'll never stop falling.

Her breath fans across my neck as I lay us both down in the now sweaty, sticky heat. We just hold each other. "I like you, Jaxal."

"Good." I kiss the top of her head. "Because I love you."

I hope you enjoyed this quick glimpse into Jaxal and Lisbel's lives! You can leave a review for their short story on Amazon.

Join my mailing list or write me personally at www.booksbyelizabeth.com/contact

Or continue the journey in another Quadrant and get Taken to Sasor…

Until then, keep falling,

Elizabeth

# Taken to Sasor
## Xiveri Mates Book 3 (Mian and Neheyuu)

They came. They shifted. They conquered. Mian expected to be made a slave by the cocky shifter barbarian and, when a rival horde takes her, discarded. But what happens when he won't give her up?

*Available in ebook or hardback on Amazon or in paperback anywhere online books are sold*

# 1

## Mian

My breath is hot against my fingers as I sit huddled, muscles straining, body clenched. My head is bowed over my knees. I try to block out the sounds of the other slaves panicking around me, but it slaps onto my skin like the sticky stain I spent all morning applying to the alehouse fence. Flimsy, weak little posts fixed together with braided reed stalks. It hadn't looked like much to begin with and the dark, oily stain hadn't helped. Now the fence is gone and all that's left of it is the black-brown ink still clinging to my arms and the fumes caught in my hair, smelling of chicory and fear.

A huge crash in the front room makes me wince. I'm dizzy with fear and hunger and thirst. *When was the last time I ate?* The fact that I can't remember does nothing but drive an agonized pang through my stomach. *Breathe. It won't matter soon. Maybe it will help. Maybe they won't want to eat skin and bones without the flesh.*

Cold seeps in through the packed dirt under my bottom. I inhale shallow breaths through my mouth, but I can still smell the other two dozen slaves' unwashed bodies beside me, even more powerful and cloying than the smell of the wood stain. More revolting. My fingers curl into the shirt sheathing me from neck to knees, the rough-spun fabric still scratchy despite having all but disintegrated. It clings to my shoulders with threads more than fabric and makes me wonder what they will take from us when they realize we have nothing to give.

Deep baritone laughter follows jests flung back and forth in a language I don't speak. The sounds, though distant *for now*, crash through my focus and behind me, one of the other slaves stifles a sob. I freeze, wondering if *they* heard it. From where I sit near the front of the group, that one little sob rings louder than the huge reed horns that trumpeted when they arrived at our gates. Gates that didn't even stand a full solar. They carved through those gates like knives through milk.

A mutinous thud slowly separates itself from the commotion in the front room. I jump, and then I jump again when it gets louder. *Footsteps? Or the panicked tattoo of my own heart?* I know what they do to the ones they find. Everyone knows the stories. *They eat humans. Flay us alive, then boil the flesh off our bones. They make great big soups out of us.*

"They're going to find us…they're going to find us!" The panicked voice at my back makes my heart clench in my throat. I glance over my shoulder and spot Sorsha over the tops of many crouched bodies trying to stand. Her brother Mika yanks her back down, but she's fighting him. Others are trying to shush them both now, and Sorsha's face is ghostly white, even in the dark. I try to swallow but my mouth is too dry and when my lips part, I inhale dust. I clap my hand over my lips, trying not to choke on it.

Mika's hand slips when Sorsha yanks again. She careens into one of the ceramic casks we stowed away in the hopes that if we did survive, one barrel of vinegar-preserved meat, a ceramic cask of bread flour, two satchels of dried fruit and three casks of water would be enough to keep us alive until we found another human settlement, or rebuilt this one. But now I see no chance of that.

As if in slow motion, Sorsha flails, hip bumping into the cask, hand flinging out to knock off the lid. It hits the packed earth with a dull clunk that rings like shattering glass.

My gaze connects with Mirabelle's, beside me. We were both sold in the last trade to this settlement. At our old settlement, we worked the grain mills together. She was really too old for that kind of work so I took on some of her chores. In exchange, she told me fantastic stories about satellites and ships and cities and great, big bodies of water from a planet once called *Earth*. Stories she says she inherited from her mother, and her mother's mother and her mother's mother's mother's mother who actually lived on the satellite that brought us to this planet.

I don't know how much of what she says is real or not, but I always liked her. A kind woman, she doesn't deserve to die here. *Do any of us?* She reaches out and takes my hand, holding it so tight I can feel the bones through her thin skin like twigs aflame, right before they turn to dust. She smiles, her half-moon lids drooping over bright blue eyes. They frighten me, those eyes. They see everything.

Mika curses, "They heard us…"

"Can we escape?"

"Where would we go?"

"Does it matter?"

"*Is* there even a way out?"

"No, the only way out is through the alehouse."

Sweet silence settles over us. It tastes like death. My vision gets fuzzy. *Fear or hunger? Have I eaten in the last solar? The last two?* I can't remember and remind myself that it doesn't matter. *Skinny humans make for crappy stew.*

Footsteps have entered the distilling room. The weight of my own breath is heavy in my lungs. It's hard to breathe. They're going to find us and skin us and boil us. Even the kids. But maybe, just *maybe*, they won't eat any of us if the offering is poor enough, and there's no offering here more abysmal than my own…

I inhale. Exhale shakily. I squeeze Mirabelle's hand just once before letting it slip from mine. Cool air brushes against my damp rear as I rise to a crouch. My head spins. *Hunger or fear? Doesn't matter. Soon it'll all be over.*

"Mian, what are you doing?" Mirabelle rasps in a voice that's barely audible.

I don't have an answer for her as I step around the bodies in my path and reach the curtain, drawing just one little corner back. I don't look behind me as I step past it into the storage room, letting the only safety I had fall shut at my back.

Silence. No one tries to pull me back in. No one comes out to sacrifice themselves at my side. *Thud.* The quiet is punctuated by the boot. It has to be a boot because it's too heavy, too forceful, to be anything else. I've never seen one of the Sasor in real life, but I've heard stories of their size. People likening them to boulders and houses and hilltops.

The storeroom is ringed in ceramic casks. I take a seat between two grain tuns, press my forehead to the gritty, bowled ceramic surface in front of me and wait for the world to settle. Then I hold my breath as the storage room door is forced open with a short, contained crack. There's a precipitous hush at my spine, but the leaden gait of a Sasori barbarian ruins it. I clench. I focus. My head spins. I nearly pass out. *Fear or hunger?* He's right on me now.

The little hope I had, more delicate than a flower, slimmer than a knife's blade, recently whetted, is filched away from me when the heavy barrel in front of me is lifted and set to the side with surprising gentleness. Goosebumps break out over my arms as I look up into his face.

He blinks and when he does, his already dark irises darken further, becoming the shadowed side of a fray leaf, glittering mahogany, but sticky and thorned. I shudder as I quickly take in the rest of him.

He wears a leather cuirass over his right side only and has similar leather plating covering his legs, but beneath that, he is all corded muscle heaped onto an enormous frame. His skin is a lighter bronze than mine is, but his hair...his hair is shocking. It's *gold*. It drapes almost to his waist on the right side, while the left is cropped close to his scalp. Against the honey of his skin, it looks...it looks like he's a male fashioned by the sun in its own image. Pretty, even if nothing else about him is. He's far too brutal-looking for that.

He's got a scar that twists away from his cheekbone, disrupting his hairline to follow the serrated line of his ear. He doesn't have an earlobe. His jaw is hard. His eyes are mean.

Without warning, he bends down and slides a massive hand through my hair. A shocking surge of laughter rises in my chest that I do my best to choke down. He's a breath away from me now, completely bent over so that I can't see anything behind him. We're face-to-face, nearly nose-to-nose.

He smells like fresh cut grass and sweat. He smells like blood above all else. Human blood. *How many has he already eaten?* A very terrible part of me I haven't met before is pleased he smells like blood. After all, maybe that mean's he's full.

His hands comb across my scalp in a way that's nearly intimate, until the gesture changes, becoming feral as he yanks me to my feet by the hair. My boneless limbs wobble like a newborn's when he sets me down. Fear and hunger war with the adrenaline, which wins out. I plant my feet and inhale blood, wood, metal and leather and I don't exhale. Can't exhale. Not when I take in the size of the alien in front of me.

His shoulders span mine three times over and his chest is as deep as my shoulders are broad. He's three heads higher than I am, maybe more. All I know is that I have to crane my neck way back to hold his gaze. And I do hold his gaze. I hold his gaze like my life depends on it, watching as the color shifts again, darkening until it's so black I can see through it to the depths of the universe.

What a funny way to go. Shipped from settlement to settlement, never staying in one long enough to find friends or family or roots. About to be killed by an alien barbarian with the universe in his eyes because a woman was nice to me once and told me funny stories about the universe. I exhale, ready, and smile.

But when his face-sized palm charges towards me again, it isn't to reach out and snap my neck or sever my spine. The brute is reaching straight for…straight for my breast! Instincts kick in and I give the back of his hand a decisive swat.

Shock.

I jump three feet out of my skin. *I just swatted him. The cannibal barbarian alien.* I meet his gaze, hold fast and watch as the most terrifying thing of all happens. His lips…they curl up, parting to reveal a flash of perfectly white, square teeth. This cannibal barbarian alien is smiling at me.

I jerk back, stumbling into the tun. I reach out to catch it, but he's already there, one hand on its smooth side, the other holding the lid in place. He rights the ceramic slowly, without releasing me from his gaze. It tracks my hand when I touch my chest. My heart seems to be trying to make a break for it, despite the fact that the rest of me is rooted in place.

Cask settled, he reaches for my palm and, catching it, tosses it aside so forcefully, I stumble again. *What's he doing?* He's looking at my…buttons. They're giant mismatched buttons that look like the buttons on doll clothes — some that I think actually did come from the dolls' clothes of the highborn mistresses — and he's *inspecting* them with an expression that suggests they just insulted his dead mother. And then he lifts a single finger and I watch in fascination and horror as a sharp, serrated point *grows* from the tip of his nail.

A finger-long at its longest, he brings that freshly formed claw down in one swift motion and slices through the loose thread anchoring my top button. My shirt falls open to the navel, exposing my bony ribcage and small breasts. I tell my body to grab it and hold it closed — *for comets' sake!* — but my body does something else.

I slap him. *Again.*

I rocket four feet into the air instead of the puny three I shot up the first time. When I land, I forget about the shirt. My arms are frozen away from my body, waiting for him to slice me open as quickly and easily as he did that piece of thread.

I wait. And I'm left waiting.

Because he touches his cheek where I hit him, blinks many times in that strange alien way, then his lips peel back and he laughs. He laughs so full and from the belly it makes razorblades appear in mine. *I can't remember ever hearing anybody laugh like that.* And he's a barbarian cannibal alien.

I jump again, shocked, when his laughter dies and he fixes me with brown eyes that are both condescending and indulgent. He shakes his head, grabs my arm and starts dragging me towards the door.

He says something to me. It sounds playful, but he could just as easily be telling me that it's time to be disemboweled now.

"Okay," I answer, knowing that whatever he means, I don't exactly have a choice in it.

He grunts out another laughter-like snort, but just as we reach the door, I hear a light cough behind me. I freeze. He freezes. He looks over his shoulder and his eyes meet mine and when he shakes his head so slow like that, the long tresses of his wavy hair tickle my bare arm.

"Tokan, ya reesa, teka annak," he says, and though I don't know the words, all I can think in response is, *human stew, here we come…*

# 2
## Neheyuu

"Tokan, ya reesa, teka annak," I tell her. *Close, but not enough.* I call her *ya reesa* — a title of honor when intended and, when sneered, a title of disrespect. Perhaps I use a little of both here when I call her brave. *Little brave one.* She *is* to defy me as she's done. I just didn't realize how brave until this moment.

How clever too.

She nearly succeeded in distracting me, and if not for the clumsiness of the humans behind the curtain, she would have.

I look upon the gaunt human faces in hiding. They are each as poorly clothed as she is, and so thin as to be considered starved by Sasor standards. Slaves. Reesa is certainly one, even if her coloring would be considered rare among the United Manerak Tribes.

Like raw bronze, she is both red and gold at the same time. She shines, even in this dim, dusky cellar, illuminated only by the outside light filtering in through uneven slats in the walls. Similar though our colors may be, that is where our likeness ends. She is a puny, runty little thing with bones like dried reeds and strange eyes that are dark and expressive. *Human.*

They are a species I have encountered before, though never as First of my tribe, and I feel a renewed rush of adrenaline and pleasure that my warriors and I have finally found and taken such a substantial number of them. It's considered a great success to come across a human tribe and decimate it.

Their females are compatible with our species and their males weak. I don't know if I've seen a human that was this pretty though, funny mannerisms and all. She hit me several times — a strange defense as she is without claws and likely a small fraction of my weight, with no warrior training at all — and now she just watches me, as if waiting for something.

Typically, I would have rutted her by now and there is no question — I *will* rut this little reesa. I reach out and touch her hair. I have never seen such a color before. As if it were stolen from the depths of an ocean, or stripped away from the stars. So black it's nearly blue. And even in filth, so *sviking* soft. I pull my hand back, wanting to touch it again — knowing that I *will* touch it again — but I allow her the chance to give to me what I seek. Because not even her matted hair, the stench of her unwashed and threadbare clothing, and the smudges of dirt and ash on her skin are enough to deter me.

"You want them to live, ya reesa?" I know she does not understand my words, so I show her what I mean. I lift a hand again for her breast but she angles away from me, shielding herself with that filthy rag I mean to tear from her body.

She says a word in a language she knows I do not speak. She shakes her head for added meaning.

"Tszk," I say, though why I tell her the word she needs to deny me, I have no idea.

Irritated with myself, I flit away her hand when she tries to block mine, and mold my palm to her chest, admiring the weight of her small tit as I hold it. It's larger than it should be given that I can see the bones of her chest through her skin, and the bones of her ribs. Her hip bones are likely to be just as prominent, and it doesn't matter. I want to see them too.

Her jaw sets, pupils contract. She pries my fingers away from her tunic and shakes her head just once, firmly. She says her strange alien word again.

"Yena," I answer. This is a better word. One she will get accustomed to saying to me, once she realizes who I am.

She does not break. I do not move. We stare one another down, silence stretched like a tanning line between us. I think it surprises her as much as me that I am the one to cede first. Irritated, I am ready to return to my warriors and enjoy the celebrations from battles easily won. I glance meaningfully at her people, huddling against one another, trying not to meet my gaze at all costs. Funny, that they cower when she does not.

Reaching among the mass of their bodies, I grab the first human I see. A female. I assume she is older given the shriveled way her skin clings to her frame. She has thick grey hair tied away from her face. Her lower lip quivers and she says something to the reesa that makes her wince.

Reesa looks from the woman to me. An expression of pain crosses her face. She takes a half-step towards me that surprises me again, then holds her wrists out between us, revealing their slightly paler insides. She is covered in black markings, sketches drawn all over her skin that will not fade.

We don't have this tradition in my tasmaran — no manerak tasmaran does — but on this little reesa, I find the markings beautiful. Though dozens of small patterns are scattered over her arms and shoulders, for now she focuses on thin, black rings just below her palms. The lines are straight, but incomplete. A small gap of clear skin tantalizes me, making me want to rub my thickest finger over it.

She speaks to me then in sentences. When I don't answer, she repeats what she has said, shaking her wrists slightly for emphasis. I don't understand her. Holding the older human by the upper arm, I again feel the front of reesa's chest, making it clear what I want. What is at stake should she refuse.

Her mouth turns down. She breaks my gaze and looks to the female. She is weighing her options. Deciding her price. And when, with the slight lowering of her chin, she agrees to pay it, I don't feel the satisfaction I thought I might. Her shoulders cave, making this already slight female seem almost insignificant. Swirling shadows, where before she was pure light.

I catch her wrist as she turns from me, my gaze roaming over the markings there and wondering about their significance. So many mysteries, beginning with why this little reesa denies me.

"Tszk," I tell her finally.

She blinks at me, her expression hollow. Lost. A deep chasm opens up at the sight of it, and I feel, for the span of a heartbeat, her mirrored emotions even though I have never felt them myself before. She is utterly transparent and through her, I can see and feel and experience everything. Beneath my true form skin, my manerak stirs slowly, as if waking up from a deep sleep.

I squeeze her breast roughly and say, "Tszk." I let her go immediately, dropping the other human female's arm as well. I push the older female slightly back and snap the curtain shut between us so that I can no longer see the human slaves, the alien barbarians.

Understanding flits across her face and she smiles at me just a little bit. Her teeth are white and straight in her small mouth, except for two on the bottom row which overlap. She doesn't have any fangs to speak of. Just reeds for bones and smiles in her eyes. Why does she smile at me when I have taken her kingdom? Mysteries. Interest. She has mine. And she has all of it.

*Dangerous.* My manerak is fully awake now, needling the underside of my skin. But I ignore it, just like I ignore any thoughts of danger in her presence. She's just a puny little human to be taken, rutted and forgotten. There's no danger here.

"Strena," I tell her. *Come.*

Her head tilts to the side, unwashed hair falling around her shoulders in matted locks. Her thin fingers still clutch her tunic together, but they no longer tremble. She glances to the heavy mud cloth hiding her humans from view.

"Tszk." I snatch up her wrist, which is thinner than the hilt of my sword and far easier to break, and lay her palm against my chest, where the leather does not bind it.

She shakes her head. I nod. Her eyes grow large in her face, making her look like she will soon transform. But humans do not have such an ability. Tszk, my little reesa is utterly transparent, totally defenseless, and mine for the taking.

I pull her roughly out of the smallest room, through the next room and finally into the main area of this shack. There, Dandena and Mor are busy brawling over a golden crown they found hidden in an ale cask. They tower over me in their manerak skins until, seeing me, they shed them and return to their true forms.

The human in my grip tugs pitifully on my arm, trying to free herself. I wonder if she's ever seen manerak before and if she hasn't, what level of terror she's currently feeling. I snort out a laugh at the thought and when I tug her forward, her heat crashes into me. *Warm. Feels nice.* I'd think her feverish if she showed any other signs of it.

She stands frozen on her feet, one hand locked in mine, the other clenched at the V of her throat. She's staring straight ahead and I follow her gaze to Mor. He licks his lips and takes a step towards us, his focus locked on her in a way that makes my skin prickle. My gaze narrows on him, sharpening, becoming lethal. *Becoming manerak.*

"What do you have there?" He says with a cocky sway of his hips. The crown forgotten, he takes a step forward. His gold hair, stained red, flutters in his wake.

"Found her hiding," I answer with a grin. Anticipation rears its restless head. My manerak opens up inside of me like a mouth.

"Was she alone?"

"Yena," I lie for reasons unknown. My fingers twitch.

"Then there is only one to be had."

"Yena."

He wipes the back of his hand across his mouth, smearing the blood of dead humans across his face. "I'd like to have her."

I laugh. "Come on then."

Mor's thick eyebrows fade back into his skin the moment the challenge is accepted. The corners of his mouth stretch back towards his hairline and I feel my pulse hammer, manerak unreasonably thrilled as it expands and elongates in response.

The little reesa jolts beside me when my shoulders begin to swell and my thighs thicken and lengthen. Already hunched over her, soon I tower. The uncomfortable wooden roof is no match for my manerak's size. It brushes the top of my head and then my shoulders, forcing me to either stoop or tear straight through it. *Do it.* But then the roof might cave, crushing her beneath it. The thought nags, and then disappears like vapor.

My manerak sizzles beneath my skin, aching with a tension that feels distinct from the way it usually does, though I'm damned to put my finger on it. *Eager.* I feel my brow bone flatten, my eyes expand, my pupils slit. My fangs come down to shield my teeth and I only release reesa when I feel claws claim my all ten of my fingertips. From between my forked tongues, I issue a hiss.

Mor charges and though he is one of my better fighters, he is still no match for me. I am First of my tribe for a reason. I wonder if his heightened bloodlust is the reason that he issues this challenge — one we both know he's going to lose — or if it has something to do with the slave beside me. Can he also see her radiance? The thought grates. My manerak seethes and spits.

She jerks wildly now, back slamming into the nearest wall. My forked tongues loll out of my mouth, tasting the air she creates. Something sour and sticky, like the tart rathra leaves used by our woodsmiths, and beneath it something sweet that makes the first wave of bitterness possible to overcome. *Blossoms. The nectar of the carnivorous egra flowers. Beautiful. Dangerous.* I release her fully and with a gentle push against her thin chest, guide her behind me so that I can have both hands free when I meet Mor in a clash of thunder.

There are no weapons in a challenge, so he swipes for me with his claws. He is a smaller male, both in his true form and in his manerak, but his strength lies in his speed. He spins away from me as I block and comes in below my arm, attempting to switch around me and bring himself closer to reesa.

My manerak call reverberates deep in my chest, causing my whole body to tremble with its might. I bring my foot down on his thigh, stopping his path. I swing my fist around to meet his cheek, drawing blood. He rises with a hiss, claw raking my ribs as he spins out of my grasp.

My manerak skin stretches, becoming broader with the tangy scent of his blood — and mine. The other warriors back to the very edges of the room, dragging casks — mostly ale — that they want to preserve with them. I attack first this time, moving straight through a flimsy piece of wood these humans once used for a table.

My shoulder connects with Mor's sternum. He tries to absorb the blow, which is his second mistake — after issuing challenge in the first place. I take him down and together we fly through the nearest wall. We land on the sand outside and before he has a chance to blink, I score his chest twice more.

"That's three times to blood, brother," I rattle, my voice distorted as I am still manerak. I push myself off of him with a grin.

He punches the packed sand angrily but still takes my hand when offered. "Challenge is to you, warrior," he says.

I yank him to his feet and feel my manerak begin to settle — at least, until I return to the shattered shed and see Dandena, Rehet and Ock closing in on my prize. I open my mouth and my manerak hiss is so deafening that I can't speak through it.

They turn, surprise etched onto their true form faces. Dandena breaks the quiet. "One blooding to three, in favor of First?"

I nod once. Dandena applauds and holds out her hand to take her winnings from the other two, who curse. I don't care for their bets, and break through the semi-circle they've made surrounding reesa. She stands with her spine still welded to one of the flimsy wooden walls. She's managed to find a knife and holds it out in front of her with two hands. She clearly has no idea how to use it, but it does look sharp. Very sharp. And it has an emerald jewel in the hilt.

"That isn't *your* blade is it, Rehet?" I balk, laughing hard enough to make my belly ache.

The others laugh too, while Rehet at least has the decency to grumble softly in shame, "She is quicker than she looks."

I inhale pride, and exhale relief when I push the males and Dandena away and see that reesa is unharmed. Her wide eyes turn up at me and I glance at the blade in her fist, shaking my head. Misunderstanding my reaction, she jumps in the air, unfurls her fingers and holds the knife out to me. She is shaking. Afraid. *She is unused to manerak.* I hiss as I feel the bones in my body contract and scale, my fangs retracting, my face slimming, my rattle dying, my shoulders narrowing, until I am finally in my true form once again.

Settled, I reach for her hand, hesitating a breath away from her fingers when she jumps, this time half a head into the air. I grin and she seems to like this because half of her mouth quirks. She still offers the knife between us but I wrap my fingers around her fingers.

"Tszk," I tell her. She won it off of Rehet. She has earned this. I press the blade back to the center of her chest and turn to the others, eager to get out of here — eager to get *her* out of here, away from the males and into my own private dolsk. "We ride now."

———

# What to read next

**Lord of Population (Population Book 1)**
When Abel comes across one of the alien overlords, she loots his corpse, the good little scavenger she is. She doesn't expect his death to be erm, temporary. He hunts her down and gives her a choice. Accept his help... The catch? She's now his.

*This is a sci-fi, fantasy, post-apocalyptic romance mashup with a guaranteed HEA and plenty of slow burn steam. Tropes include enemies-to-reluctant allies-to-lovers, found family, he falls first, he rescues her, she rescues him, she has a nightmare, "who did this to you", one bed*

**The Hunting Town (Twisted Fates Book 1)**
Drugs, cartels, the mafia. Pain, greed, and revenge. These are what Plumeria brought with her when she took a new job tending bar in the fighting pits outside of town – fighting pits owned by five men, known as the Brothers. Knox wouldn't have put anything before his brothers – not even his own life – until he met Mer. But when her life is put at risk, he intervenes, dragging his entire family into her world.

*This is a romantic suspense featuring two couples that both reach their HEA. The first couple are two cage fighters, the second a medical student turned exotic dancer and the grump who owns the club. Plenty of steam and mayhem await.*

**Dark City Omega (Berserker Kings Book 1)**
There are three absolutes for any Omega who has the misfortune of finding herself in Paradise Hole:

The first - stay away from the cities.
The second - stay off the road.
The third - stay away from Alphas.

Echo knew the rules. She just never expected to be hunted by a lord among Alphas, by a Berserker himself, the savage of Dark City. But he's been on her scent for six weeks.

And now, he's found her.

*Coming soon, this is an action-packed dark fantasy romance ripe with spice, magic, and battles and perfect for fans of diverse books, possessive heroes and strong lady leads. Tropes include omegaverse, enemies-to reluctant allies-to lovers, fated mates-ish, one sleeping mat, trek through the forest together, she's injured, he saves her, she saves him, grumpxgrump*

# All Books by Elizabeth

**Berserker Kings - Enemies to lovers. With magic.**
Dark City Omega, Book 1 (Echo and Adam)
*more to come!*


**Population - Battles and Heroes that Bite.**
Lord of Population, Book 1 (Abel and Kane)
Monster in the Oasis, Book 2 (Diego and Pia)
Immortal with Scars, Book 3 (Lahve and Candy)
more to come!


**Twisted Fates - Mafia. Brotherhood. Murder.**
The Hunting Town, Book 1 (Knox and Mer, Dixon and Sara)
The Hunted Rise, Book 2 (Aiden and Alina, Gavriil and Ify)
The Hunt, Book 3 (Anatoly and Candy, Charlie and Molly)


**Xiveri Mates - Aliens. Heat. New Worlds.**
Taken to Voraxia, Book 1 (Miari and Raku)
Taken to Nobu, Book 2 (Kiki and Va'Raku)
Exiled from Nobu, Book 2.5, a Novella (Lisbel and Jaxal)
Taken to Sasor, Book 3 (Mian and Neheyuu) *standalone
Taken to Heimo, Book 4 (Svera and Krisxox)
Taken to Kor, Book 5 (Deena and Rhork)
Taken to Lemora, Book 6 (Essmira and Raingar)
Taken by the Pikosa Warlord, Book 7 (Halima and Ero)
*standalone
Taken to Evernor, Book 8 (Nalia and Herannathon)
Taken to Sky, Book 9 (Ashmara and Jerrock)
Taken to Revatu, Book 10, A Novella (Latanya and Grizz)
*standalone

# Collections

**Xiveri Mates - Aliens. Heat. New Worlds.**
Collection 1: Books 1-3 + Exiled from Nobu
*More to come!*

# Audiobooks

**Xiveri Mates - Aliens. Heat. New Worlds.**
Taken to Voraxia, Book 1 (Miari and Raku)
Taken to Nobu, Book 2 (Kiki and Va'Raku)
Taken to Sasor, Book 3 (Mian and Neheyuu) *standalone
*More to come!*

# French Language

**Passion Xiveri : Unis Pour La Vie – Des extraterrestres. De la sensualité. De nouveaux mondes.**
Capturée par le Roi de Voraxia, tome 1 (Miari et Raku)
Convoitée par le Seigneur de guerre de Nobu, tome 2 (Kiki et Va'Raku)
Kidnappée par le Métamorphe de Sasor, tome 3 (Mian et Neheyuu) *l'intrigue se situe hors du Quadrant 4
*D'autres livres seront bientôt publiés !*